City Smells

A Collection of Writing By

Alice Shin	Rachelle Hafen
Alec Ross	Sarah Rose Etter
Kevin Lucia	Symonne Torpy
Wendy Swearingen	Jewels Johnson
Digby Beaumont	Charlotte Scadeng
Dewi Putri Kirana	Nii Amu Swaniker
Mike Ripley	Alicia Hoffman
Stephanie Daniels	Rachel Lisi
Matthew Rhodes	Dan Beck
R. A. Davis	Adam "Bucho" Rodenberger
Pete Botman	Caroline Dotson
Brooke LeBlanc	James Meredith
Ravis Harnell	Graeme Sandford
Ada Spark	Chris Lee Ramsden
Karen Jones	Kelly Smith
Jane Bratton	Phillip Lawrence
Leslie Joseph	Patrick Browning
Lin Robinson	

Edited by
Sean Merrigan

For all the writers who followed their nose.

Contents

Stories

Foreword
by Sean Merrigan

I always thought the air would be cleaner beyond the edge of the city. That was probably one of the things I said to convince myself it was a good idea to move in with her. But in those four months all I discovered was that at the edge of London, all the smells you would expect - from the rich mulch of wooded lanes to the vestiges of rural Buckinghamshire - were stifled and flat beneath the exhaust fumes generated by that grand, orbital hymn to combustion: the M25. Round and round, a psychotic circuit of burning rubber and Magic Trees. People sliding around the perimeter. Going nowhere.

After everything was said and done, I hired a gas-guzzling monster of my own, and with the help of my friend Pauly, was packed and gone by lunchtime. 'Let's be out of here before she gets home from work,' he'd said. Too right. In an hour we were barrelling down the A40, back into the heart of my festering, poisonous and beloved city. We skirted Mayfair, Piccadilly and Westminster. Not for us the synthetic waft of expensive brands and chain coffee shops, our trajectory was south east, over Vauxhall Bridge, and on toward the raw mix of South London.

I found the first few molecules of lamb patty somewhere around Camberwell; at the lights in Peckham, a smidgin of skunk from a reclining bike messenger. As we hit New Cross gate I caught a powerful blast of stale beer from the doorway of the New Cross Inn. It was the olfactory equivalent of someone switching on the lights. I was home.

Five hours later I was standing by the benches in Point Hill park, Greenwich, savouring my favourite view over the city. I was with Phil, a fellow writer, walker and stalwart drinking companion. We'd been in every pub from Lee Green up to Blackheath Village, some of the rankest, most pungent establishments still able to command a license. As we'd sat drinking and talking about my recent romantic entanglement, I soaked up that redolent fug as enthusiastically as I soaked up the pints of porter: dark, bitter ale mixed with the smell of damp rolling tobacco and fag smoke; a waft of body odour with highlights of chalk dust from the dartboard. Walking across the heath towards Point Hill I'd caught a faint tang, salty and damp, rising gently up from the river and blowing south across the suburbs.

'What will you miss most, when you move to Copenhagen?' Phil asked me as we stood there, watching the evening descend into the twinkling basin beneath us. 'This view?'

I thought for a minute. 'No. This smell'

Sean Merrigan
Copenhagen, December 2008

Flash Fiction

Fashion District
By Alice Shin

Summer's heat hovered like an abuela's hug - soft, suffocating and unrelenting.

'Coca-Cola, one-dollar!'

Hotdogs wrapped in bacon sizzled alongside slivers of sweet, browning onion. Every few feet, vendors were selling eight-ounce hunks of pineapple and guava skewered on wooden dowels. Sweating children were placated with golden globes of salted mango, fresh juice dripping cool and sticky down their arms.

Alma wanted to grab a handful of melting ice from one of the fruit stands and rub it all over her neck.

'Ma, what if I pay half? I'll pay half.'

'You think I'ma lechu pay a hundred-and-fifty dollar for a dress on sale?'

If it was waiting for her in an air-conditioned venue with sanitary dressing rooms, then yes, yes, and yes.

Alma tried again. 'It's my money, Ma.'

'You wan walk to mall? Your choice.'

They had been on foot for about forty-five minutes, every flat carrying a million copies of the same nine dresses. Racks of fuchsia, gold, and lavender were vomiting miles of wasted fabric, each space as claustrophobic as the next.

Above almost every shopping flat was a second floor that appeared to have no access to the first. No visible signs of fire escapes or elevators connected the two stories. The only sign that anything happened upstairs at all were the iron bars jailing each window.

Alma pulled a rectangle of catalogue paper from her back pocket and unfolded it. There it was, that turquoise satin-and-tulle Jessica McClintock gown with silver beading and a sweetheart neckline. How could anything as beautiful as this be found in such a crowded and dirty-looking place?

A hand reached out and snatched the glossy paper from her hand.

'Going to prom? What size are you? A four? A two? Let's try a four,' said a woman with fried auburn hair and brown lipstick.

A pair of hands stripped her down to her underwear and enveloped her in layer upon layer of cool, turquoise satin.

'Ma-!' Alma uttered.

But the hands weren't listening. Instead, they spun her around and pushed her towards a dusty mirror.

'Pretty girl, look at that.'

It was her dress. And it fit. And it was beautiful.

The woman handed Alma back her catalogue slip and pointed to her reflection in the mirror. Friendly smile, 'Same dress, yeah?'

'It doan fit right.'

Alma turned to face her mother. How could she betray her like that?

But the saleswoman remained as sweet as the smell of her pan-stick make-up. 'You jus' need a padded bra for your cositas, but otherwise perfect, yeah?' Outstretched palm. 'Sixty, cash.'

'Forty-five.'

Alma wanted to cry.

A truck paused, and then gunned its engine in front of the store.

A smoking trail of gasoline was left to permeate the space, destined to become trapped within the fibers of the unsold fabric.

More Than Cherry Blossoms
By Alec Ross

'You can call me the Garbage Collector, but it's not what you think. I don't work for the city. I don't go from house to house picking up trash. No. What I'm about to do is far worse.'

He pulls out a gun and screws on a silencer.

'You see, the reason I'm calling myself the Garbage Collector is really quite simple. I take care of garbage: garbage such as you. Real garbage collectors will eventually find you. The smell of rotten flesh is hard to ignore.' Pause. His eyes drift to the nearby trash bags. 'It's all in the smell. As gross and disgusting as the trash can be, it's nothing compared to the reek of maggot-infested human meat. It's not exactly the kind of smell that the city wants.'

He raises the gun with a steady hand and takes aim at the bound and gagged man in front of him. The man tries to scream but manages only a muffled whimper. Tears roll from the man's eyes.

For the Garbage Collector, it's never personal. He only has a name, or a photo. He knows who the person is, but he doesn't need nor want the details. This keeps it simple.

He pulls the trigger.

STOP

The National Mall. He makes it a point to come out in early April every year for the Cherry Blossom Festival. The rich, rose-like aroma of the nearly pure white blossoms has always overwhelmed him. Like a strong perfume. There's really no wonder why the blossoms are so important in Japan. Everyone talks about how pure the blossoms are - how they symbolize a fresh start. He sees the pink that radiates from the petals that only last a week. They're not that pure; especially with the thousands of people who defile the trees by climbing and ripping away the petals.

This year he walks the long path and tries to ignore the people who push and shove just to get the perfect shot. They don't realize that it isn't the image that's important. No, it's the smell.

This is the smell of the city. These flowers that only last a week.

So many have tried to describe the scent, but no one has ever been able to capture what it is to him. It smells of spring. Of life, but not fresh beginnings: merely the cycle.

The dead man decomposes two miles from here. His scent is the counter. Both are necessary, even if it's not what the city wants.

*

He grabs a copy of the Post. The front cover has two predominant photos. One shows the cherry blossoms with children smiling, flying kites. The other is the man he shot. His body is still recognizable. The paper calls the dead man a violent sexual predator. He calls him garbage. The city already smells better.

Last Rite
By Kevin Lucia

Damn. Here I am on my knees holding my guts in with my hands, and all I think about is how this city smells.

'Shit!' Paul grabs my shoulder. I wince. 'Goddamn, Sollie…hold on brother. Meatwagon's comin'!'

Meatwagon. Makes me think of Ballpark hotdogs roasting at Tony's Texas Hots, one the few food vendors still brave enough to work the streets all hours. I'll miss smelling the onions he roasts on the side; the slaw, that tangy scent of his secret recipe relish - miss it badly, damn it.

'All units; please respond,' drones the canned voice of the squad car CB, 'officer down….'

Something shifts under my hands, puffs out the unpleasant, coppery scent of blood and the acrid smell of burnt flesh, along with something rotten; like spoiled meat left in the sun. Reminds me of times Paul and I found dead bodies dumped at the city landfill.

The pressure on my shoulder increases. Bet Paul's about to pass the hell out, right next to me. 'God, they're comin' Sollie; hold on...'

My nostrils quiver, arms tremble like limp spaghetti. Won't be long until I take my last nose dive, literally.

I love the smell of city traffic; gasoline and exhaust mixed with just the right touch of burnt oil. Reminds me of the car races dad and I saw. Every Saturday he and I went to Five Mile, a dirt track out in the country. Gasoline, exhaust, oil always takes me back. I love the smell more than those Texas Red Hots.

I catch a whiff of myself, almost throw-up. I'm covered in sour, fear-smelling sweat, and something intimately familiar – burnt ozone of a spent firearm: hot, sharp in my nostrils.

Something gurgles under my hand. That's pretty much my last hurrah. Somehow, as I sag to the ground, I force myself over on my back. At least my guts'll stay where they belong, and Paul's last sight of me wouldn't have intestines pooling around his feet.

I sigh, relax against the pavement. My eyes close, and the world goes dark. I'm happy to be on my back, guts still inside me....

Wait. I smell one last thing.

Rain. Clean, crisp; falls slowly at first – drops, sprinkles, drizzles, then comes faster. It smells pure, fresh, and thank God....clean.

Storm Drenched Harlot
By Wendy Swearingen

When I was wild and young you were my favorite playmate. I ran to you in joy and sorrow and, always, you unfurled your wanton streets before me.

I remember my final visit with you the best. You intoxicated me, tempted me with the chaos of your evening scents. On one street, the aroma of savory gumbo mingled with honeysuckle and beer. I dug in my pockets only to find them empty, and, sighing, walked on. This time into the rich smell of strong coffee mingled with fresh beignets, new leather and strawberry daiquiris. I was filled with longing for things I couldn't have.

So I moved on again, but the jazzman on the corner played a mournful song. It sounded like heartbreak, and I felt he played just for me. Or was it you? I told him I was sorry I had no money to drop into his trumpet case, but he only smiled and played a jaunty tune that set my feet moving again.

You've loved everyone who has ever loved you, but only a little. They didn't call you easy for nothing, and I had little to offer. I wanted to stay forever, yet knew I had to go. Did you watch me leaving? Did you miss me at all?

Since then you've known harder times. Drowned and scarred, abandoned. Where have all your suitors gone? Only your most constant lovers have stayed. Your beautiful streets are littered with chemical-soaked refuse. Surely, the scent of your heartbreak masks all else. So much of you is dark, silent, and full of threat. I want to return and remind you of my affections. I adore you as I always have, perhaps more for your fall from grace. I wonder could you love me back now?

Now that we are the same?

Nature Boy
by Digby Beaumont

'Step out of the car, with your hands up … I said out of the car, or I'll shoot.'

The man opens the door and stands, squinting in the powerful beam of light. 'Is there a problem, Officer?'

'Your name, please, sir?'

'It's Pink, Officer. Felix Pink.'

'Date of birth?'

'The third of November, 2057.'

The patrolman punches the man's details into his PDA. 'Mind telling me what you're doing out here at this time of night, Mr Pink?'

'I've been for a walk, Officer.'

'A walk?'

'Yes.'

'Where exactly?'

'In the forest.'

'A walk in the forest? And why would you want to do that, sir? The official city walkways not to your liking?'

Felix clears his throat. 'No, they're fine. Really. It's just, I felt like a change of scene, that's all. Thought I'd come out here, breathe in the air.' He shields his eyes against the glare of the light.

'Keep your hands up, sir.'

'Sorry, Officer.'

The patrolman moves closer. 'It's not what you'd call normal behaviour, is it, sir?'

'I'm not breaking any law, Officer, am I?'

'Thanks to Urban Deodorization, the city offers a cornucopia of designated fragrances to enjoy. Ocean Breeze, Alpine Meadow, Tropical

Bloom, Potpourri … all enriched with a range of essential vitamins and minerals.'

'Yes, but—'

'So why, I ask myself, would anyone want to come and assault their senses out here? A right-thinking individual would find the idea repellent.' He sniffs. 'So, how often do you engage in this type of activity, sir?'

'Not that often, really.'

'What do your wife and family make of it?'

'I'm not married, Officer. And I have no family. I live alone.'

The patrolman's PDA beeps. He reads the display then looks back at the man. 'Right, Mr Pink. Take my advice, stick to the city in future. The forest is no place for a law-abiding citizen.'

'Right, Officer.'

The patrolman waits for the man to drive away and returns to the patrol car. But he doesn't get in behind the wheel. He reaches inside and switches off all the lights then sets off into the forest on foot, along a narrow, dirt track.

Some distance on, he stands motionless. Eyes closed, his face softens as he draws in the pine and fern-scented air and holds it for a few seconds before letting it stream out.

The Smell of Her Drowned City
By Dewi Putri Kirana

She never knew that smells could make her feel so lonely.

She has not realized it until this day, how many smells she has dismissed as trivial daily facts: the oily aroma from the kitchen when her maid makes fried rice for the family breakfast; the sharp cologne filling the bathroom after her father has used it; the soft apple perfume of her car, which always accompanies her on the way to work.

And when she goes out for a morning jog, she will take for granted the slightly fetid sewer, the choking exhaust fumes of early car users, and occasionally the sweet whiff of flowers and fruits from her neighbors' gardens.

But now all have gone, swallowed by the merciless, damp reek of mud.

She stands on the second floor of her house, gazing at the endless floodwater. Earlier this morning, gas had been leaking out of her drowned little car, sending a nauseating odor throughout the surroundings. But now even that stench has faded away to nothingness.

It is unfair because she knows, at the other side of the city, people are complaining about the strong tang of midday sun beating down on asphalts, criticizing the tasty aromas of their own hot food, while she sits alone, inhaling the cold scent of water in her corner of the city

If the water goes down, there will be new smells in her town. The garbage piling high on roads, sewers, and rivers. The rotten vegetables and meats in her refrigerator. The smells of sadness, hopelessness and anger that will befall the metropolis.

The new wind brings down the scent of rain. She looks at the faraway darkening sky then down to the empty buckets at her side. Clean water has long since run out, and now she is depending on the water from above.

She does not know whether to cherish or to weep at the incoming downpour.

The Stench
By *Mike Ripley*

'This is it.'

A hush fell over Main Street; not even a murmur as people gathered round the manhole.

'Everyone move back.'

Barry Gibbons waved his arms wildly. There was a commotion as those at the front stepped back, causing those behind to do likewise.

Eventually it died down so that the only sound was the howling of the wind.

'I'll need a crowbar.'

Somebody towards the rear grabbed one from Barry's truck, passing it along until it finally arrived at the front. Barry held it aloft like Arthur, having pulled Excalibur from the stone. Everybody knew Barry, the town handy man, so nobody complained when he took charge

'Here goes.'

With a low grating sound, followed by a loud clatter, he popped the manhole cover. The whiff became overwhelming, hitting everybody like a malodorous tsunami. People used whatever they could to keep out the smell.

It started some weeks ago, but people just assumed it was the odour of manure in the country air. However, it grew stronger, despite farmers insisting they were not muck spreading. Eventually, the mayor had to act; his first test since being elected. So far, the new community centre was still a dream, the library was still lacking books and the park swings were still rusty and seatless.

'Horse shit,' declared Barry, holding his nose. 'The sewer is overflowing with manure.'

Several farmers shifted uneasily, and some people were already looking at them suspiciously.

'I promise that we will get to the root of this faecal fiasco.'

The crowd turned as one to see the mayor standing with them.

'We shall clean up this mess, and do it without hitting your pockets.'

A cheer went up.

'We shall cart this shit from our town and mark today as a public holiday.'

There was a collective hurrah.

Suddenly, the road shuddered as if hit by an earthquake. A new, foul-smelling wave oozed out of the sewer.

'This isn't a problem,' insisted the mayor.

The street shook again.

'I will see to it that this gets cleaned up.' He had to shout over the rumbling. 'We will work flat out to remove this filth from under our town.'

The sound became a deafening roar and people withdrew from the street leaving the mayor on his own.

'People, I swear,' he yelled, 'I will not raise taxes to pay for this. I will DEFINITELY not divert funds from other projects.'

A crack appeared in the road. It spread down the middle, causing the surface to shear, creeping up on the unsuspecting mayor.

'The welfare of this town is my main concern.'

The road opened up beneath him, sending up a brown-green shower of shit causing many to retch and vomit. Onlookers watched in horror as the mayor disappeared into the slurry running through the sewers.

Beer and Propane
By Stephanie Daniels

Sure, there was the usual cigarette sting still left in my hair and passing wisps of burnt rubber-laced exhaust fumes, but this morning there was also a different stench in the air.

It was the smell of 10,000 fuzzy yellow bees on a quest to find a hive; the smell of a new chapter in a freshly printed, un-creased book; a refreshing splash of spring mud on the back of your blue jeans.

The Starbucks dark roast dueled in the streets with the bagel shop. Red rover, red rover, baker's bread! Caffeine is coming over!

Someone is saturated with patchouli. If you lived in the 1960s you probably think it's the girl in the purple prairie skirt. It's actually the girl with the over-sized non-functioning red belt trying desperately to be chic. Forty years ago she would have been an unshowered hippie.

In the city you forget the smells you used to know. Wet, gooey, smashed worms after heavy rain. Crisped, fresh firewood in the night. Pine trees sweating in the heat.

These days it's cardboard pine trees hanging from rearview mirrors. A gas leak from the wind's dance with the pilot light in the stove. The patches of dirt repeatedly urinated on by two giant rottweilers and one wrinkly pug.

You can actually catch particles of cement in your nose hairs as you dust past a downtown construction site. On State Street you desperately try to separate the smell of chocolate from cheese corn and armpit rot.

Your own armpit is pretty bad, but not that bad.

On the train there's no escape from the smell of 2,896,016 prior asses on worn seats. Someone save me, quick! You say to yourself.

There's a moment of panic before the doors chop open and reveal saffron and curry from under the tracks.

You think about it for a minute. Curry, I mean. Curry could be for dinner. But then the undertones of baked fish from the African joint make you realize it's probably not a good idea.

The entire walk back you try to dodge certain scents. Sometimes the beer patio makes your stomach turn into a knot. Not today.

Today it's time for beer and propane.

City Smells
By Matthew Rhodes

An elderly woman swept up cat food with quick swipes of her broom. A buzz sounded and she stepped swiftly out of the kitchen, making sure not to crunch any unswept food.

'Hold on, I'm comin',' she whispered as a second buzz sounded.

'Hello?' She asked her intercom.

'Well, how do you do Margie,' a woman said, her voice flailing affably.

'Come on up, Eileen.' She walked back to the kitchen and tossed the pile of food into the wastebasket.

'Archibald, you stupid cat,' she said as Eileen jingled into the apartment.

'Hey girl, who you talkin' to?'

'Myself. That damn cat turned its bowl over again.'

'You aren't rid of that thing yet?'

'Nope. I just don't have the heart, Eileen. Here, gimme that coat. I'll go put the kettle on.' Marge put the coat in the closet. She grabbed the kettle and put it on the stove top. As her pilot light clicked, Eileen walked in.

'Boy, there were some strong fumes out there in the hall.'

'Oh yeah?'

'Yeah, smelled like some chemicals. Very odd smell,' Eileen said. She walked to the living room and took a seat.

'Must be that moron janitor up to something.'

'That old goat ain't fired yet? The super must have a heart 'bout like yours,' Eileen said cackling over phlegm.

'We're a pitiful bunch, aren't we? Did I tell you about the Thompson family's boy?'

'What, little Frederick? What's that boy up to?'

'His mama caught him growing pot a few weeks ago,' she said as she poured hot water over two tea bags.

'You're kiddin'!'

'Nope. He had it sittin' right there on his windowsill.'

'What happened to that kid? Heck, we used to walk him to church every Sunday.'

'I don't have a clue, Eileen,' said Marge as she handed Eileen her tea.

'The more I try to figure it out, the less I know.' Marge sat across from Eileen, and dipped her tea bag in the steaming water a few times.'Y'know, Eileen, I'm beginning to smell those fumes.'

'Yeah. Smells like cat piss, pardon my French.'

'My my, I'm gonna step out and see what in the world that is.' She set her tea down, walked to her door and out of the apartment. She heard a little commotion coming from below, and headed down the stairs. She saw the Thompson's apartment door ajar, and Freddie Thompson, with red-orange eyes, being escorted out by police.

'What were you thinking, cooking meth? We're going to have to clear out this whole building,' said the officer.

'When I smoked it,' Freddie said in a gravelly whisper, 'it didn't have a smell.'

Marge rubbed her fingers on her forehead and marched back up the stairs.

'The more I try to figure it out,' she mumbled to herself, 'the less I know.'

Dashes
By R. A. Davis

I brought a new book of stories to read you. On the contents page there is a list of authors, with brackets beside the names: the year they were born, the year they died. Then their life, signified by a dash. For the ones who are still alive there is just the year of their birth and the dash. But the distance between the brackets is the same; after the dash there is a space where, if you wanted to, you could fill in the death-year. That little hyphen, striking horizontally left to right, as if through time, is the same length for everyone, unlike real lives. For our lines, there's only been a little overlap. Two lines of the same length overlapping, so the un-overlapping part is the same length for both of us. Now that you're really dying, I wonder who you might have been before me and who I might be after you.

'It's good to see you,' you say, under the coma and the closed eyes. Your machine beeps at me, forever agreeing. I sit down and begin. I wonder if you can hear me. The thought of how bored you would be if you couldn't is too frightening. To be confined to yourself, confined to a room. They always called you the Outdoor Type. It's not right you had to come to the city to die. You must always be wondering about the weather back home; if there's still snow on the hills. I got so worried you were bored I brought you a radio and left it on in your room, so you wouldn't be lonely and maybe you would hear the weather forecast. The night-nurse told me off the next day. Waste of electricity, she said. If the radio wastes electricity, what are all these other machines doing?

Beep, beep it goes, drawing the same jagged picture of a mountain peak and flat valley over and over. In the absence of the radio I've started leaving things for you to smell, so the smells are with you when I can't be. Can you smell that? That's daffodils of course. I'll bring new flowers soon. Now the days are getting warmer the nurses can open your window. Sorry for the draft, but it beats air-conditioning. Maybe you can pretend the car fumes are logs on a campfire. That wet concrete is mountain granite.

I'll read you a new story now, of mountaineers. You can dream you're striding up that mountain with them. Dream that you have reached the highest summit. Do you want to come down to the concrete and the cars, to the city and these machines? If you want me to, I'll stop there. Remember, you're the Outdoor Type. You never wanted to come home, even after the mountain had been climbed. If you want, we'll leave the story there. Beep mountain valley, beep mountain valley, valley, valley.

Of Dogs and Men
By Pete Botman

Wanted: People with a Nose. Company offering $5/hour to test odours. Must pass selection process.

The coffee in the corner snack bar was already stale. The newspaper was a day old. A sip of the thick, dark liquid helped slide the grating traffic exhaust down the back of my throat. The slot addict smoked a candied bitumen roll-up and coughed out a spit-spattered mushroom cloud at two cherries and a lemon.

I had some odd jobs running but could always use more money. I had a nose. I guess I qualified. I phoned the number in the ad and made an appointment. They gave me a mask to breathe through. It was connected to a gas canister on the other side of a partition whose valves someone was adjusting.

'I don't smell anything.'

The scientist nodded.

'Wait, now I do. This smells familiar. Did someone just fart?'

The scientist nodded again and clicked a key on his computer.

I had passed the selection process and was 'out in the field.' In the hallway of a housing tenement I recognized Masala curry mix and sunflower oil reheated a time too many. The scientist had a hand-held computer in one hand and knocked at a door with the other. An old man in a sagging vest, nostalgic with old labour, led us into the kitchen. I sniffed. Brilliantine, sweaty socks and periodontitis. And something else.

'Did you leave the gas on?' I asked.

The scientist nodded. He flicked his lighter. The flame flared extra large although it was adjusted to the minimal setting.

'I'd open the windows before smoking if I were you.' It wasn't my place to say anything, but the scientist nodded while working the stylus over his hand-held.

The old story goes like this: a man turns on the gas oven to kill himself. An hour and a bottle of whiskey later, he gets impatient that he's still alive. He pulls out a cigarette to kill the time. Boom! Mission accomplished - but not quite the way he intended. The upshot is: gas is flammable, it won't asphyxiate you. They scent the gas to make leaks detectable. The story is often told. I wonder if it is really true.

'Can't you train dogs to do this?' I ask the scientist after they pay me for a day's sniffing.

'They're too expensive' The scientist smiles.

The next morning in the snack bar, the only thing stinking is my self-esteem. The coffee is less sour. The traffic fumes cling lower to the pavement. The fruit machine junkie keeps his smell to himself.

Stalactites
By Brooke LeBlanc

His roof leaked. Beads of water collected above us like sweat in the bloated weight of humid air. I kept one eye open, keenly fixed on a single drop - a crystal disc that formed the center of a bloom of brown muck.

A dingy taint of mold mingled with the heavy wet dog smell of the city after summer rain. Scent clouds churned in the air above us, mixing with the lingering hint of cannabis and curry scraps left in the bottom of takeout boxes. I could close my eyes right now and smell it again, that strange sweet aroma of coconut and lime. They say that scent is the greatest link to memory. Well, I would know his smell anywhere – the cool tang of dead menthol Marlboros and road grit.

When I really opened my eyes, I saw that there wasn't just one leak. There were several. A steady drip-drip splashing against the bare wood floor. A puddle was forming near the crooked silver rabbit ears that served as a makeshift antennae on top of the grungy TV. Rainwater tears were scattered all over the mottled expanse of the ceiling like stalagmites.

'…Like what?'

I hadn't realized that I had spoken out loud.

'Uh, stalagmites,' I said, raising a hand like I was pointing out constellations.

'That's what they look like.'

'No. Stalactites,' he corrected while stretching out in a feline motion. 'They hold on tight, but the stalagmites push up with all their might. Remember?'

As he spoke, he moved his arms like a dance, teaching me. Fingers fluttering down like the drizzle of the itsy bitsy spider's rain spout – the stalactites, I guessed. Muscles rippled as he raised his arms, pushing up with all of his might.

I might've blushed. It was too dark for either one of us to know. Maybe I was surprised. He didn't look like the type that would know anything about geology.

'I – I think you're right.'

He turned over, wordlessly, exposing a golden, freckled back to me. He thought he was right, too.

I slipped out from under the sheets, vaguely embarrassed.

I swear I wanted to take him out of that shack with its cold floors and its crying walls. Sometimes I had foolish, romantic notions about a man that looked like he didn't know anything about geology, or Shakespeare, or da Vinci but might have known if I asked him. Sometimes I had foolish, nagging notions that he deserved better than the life he was wasting away, stuck on the underbelly of the city.

'You ever just want to leave this place? Ever want to…stay with me?'

I heard a snort, then words muffled against the pillow.

'Course not. What would your wife say?'

My water drop, the one I had been staring at for quite some time, finally pitched itself from the ceiling. Falling, like a dying cloud.

The Ferryman
by Ravis Harnell

'Is this the one?'

Keller had been standing in the shaft of light for maybe two minutes, motionless but for his upturned head, which swiveled back and forth slowly like a purposeful radar dish. Stacy watched an upside-down Crocodiles baseball cap float by her left calf and ride the filthy water eight feet further, until it passed their guide and floated into the darkness.

'Keller?

She wanted to scream, throw up, lay down in the sludge and sleep forever.

'Cotton. Sweat. Electrical fire.' He was talking to himself; she barely heard him over the unending susurrus of swiftly flowing sludge. 'The Watterson Fabrics warehouse.'

Keller turned his bright psychotic eyes and talented nose to the group.

'No. Three more manholes, maybe four.'

The slouched thing that had once been the world's leading authority on quality cheeses moved on. Stacy followed, along with the small group she'd begun to think of as her own personal version of the cast of Gilligan's Island: incompetent alpha male, check; incompetent beta male, check; rich douche bag, check; rich douche bag's wife, check; useless scientist, check. She hadn't yet figured out whether she was supposed to be Ginger or Mary Ann, and fervently hoped to be rid of the lot of them before that particular epiphany struck.

At least some of the streetlights were still on. Every hundred yards or so, Keller would do his impression of an angel, handing out proclamations while bathed in light:

'Singed fur - Addams' Pet Mart.'

'Fused glass. Must be Springton's.'

'Fresh bread. Less charred flesh. We're close.'

The Skipper began to lose his nerve.

'You know you only get paid if you get us there, right?'

Keller watched him knead his military hat from yet another pool of brilliance.

'If I led you long enough, Captain, you'd drop from nervous exhaustion and I'd have my payday in any case,' their guide said. 'Fortunately, I'm a man of my word, and we're here.'

The group sloshed forward, spent, towards the light and the ladder.

'I believe,' said Keller, 'there was the matter of my payment?'

A Crown Royal bag was pushed forward into Stacy's hands. She gave it to the prim little gnome, who poured its contents into an open palm and counted the bones with excruciating care. Finally, Keller secreted the payment, climbed the rusted rungs of rebar, and pried aside the manhole with a special tool.

Halfway up, they could all smell the coffee.

Non-fiction

Renie, This One's For You
By Ada Spark

Renie's second-floor window was a prime spot for observing the Cowley Road loonies. She'd been renting the placeit from the council since the fifties, she said. When I went to see the room, she'd hauled all seventy-eight years of herself up two flights of original mahogany balustrade and announced that I was the first lady she'd had in the house. It was nice to be a lady for once. My college romance had fizzled out after finals and I was, technically, homeless, so I overlooked the king-sized burn on the single mattress, the orange varnished Anaglypta and the psycho lying in wait across the corridor., I and paid her a whole week's rent in advance...

I didn't see much of Renie for the first couple of months. I was busy nursing a broken heart and fending off unwelcome nocturnal visits from David across the hall. I'd venture downstairs from time to time for tokens: the electrics and the gas stove in the second floor kitchen were still powered by shilling meters. There was a tang in the air even then – an all-pervasive signature scent provided mainly by Renie's cat, Timmy, who perched on her shoulder like an obese orange parrot. He and laughed in the face of litter trays. She'd got hundreds of shillings bagged up in her sideboard, but the exchange rate was a sensitive issue. It depended on the weather, the decade in which she was living on that particular day, and whether I was game for a trip to Boots to pick up her incontinence pads.

When Weird David did a moonlight flit, leaving six months' unpaid rent and countless empty tubes of Germolene in his wake, everything changed. Even the bookbinder who rented the attic room came down to celebrate his departure with a mug of tepid ginger wine. He was a timid soul, so frightened of David that he locked himself in his garret when he knew he was at home. Renie had berated him some ten years previously for spending too much time in the shower, and he was still paying her an extra twenty-seven pence a week by standing order. He ate seven cherry tomatoes every day, steeping them in boiled water for an hour beforehand to drive off the chemicals.

The spare room wasn't empty for long. Four days after David left, I was careless enough to leave a one night stand in my bed and go to work. Renie tried to decapitate him with a wicker carpet beater at first: she'd passed him in the hall whilst making a rare foray onto the landing and assumed that he was from the council. They'd got chatting, apparently, and by the time I got home he'd moved in. He was older than me, with a HND from the Poly, but he had a double futon and could cook.

And oh! How very good he was in the kitchen. We fanned our flame with Eggs Benedict, glazed lamb shanks, spiced kumquats and Manchego cheese and the sheets got sticky with croissant crumbs. The air hung thick with the velvet fug of sauteed garlic, punctuated by an occasional swatch of lemon, or toasted almond. On Friday nights, Timmy would lie in wait at the top of the stairs, drunk on the prospect of Dover sole. We'd spend the few hours our appetites could spare us gazing out of the window at the army of eccentrics who patrolled the street below.

'It seems sinful' said Prince Charming one evening, over the moules mariniere, 'to feed the cat, when Renie's eating those bloody awful ready-meals.'

Before long we were ferrying trays up and down the stairs. Renie would regale us with tales of her lodgers, her lovers and house parties so wild they shook the ceilings. We reciprocated with gigantic plates of pasta alla puttanesca and glasses of Vouvray. We knew no portion control. She stayed slight, but the plates always came back clean. As July squeezed into August, we started to suffocate. A nauseating musk was rising from Renie's rooms. There was always a top note of cat and last night's dinner, but the base scent was soft, rotting.

Her daughter 'phoned. 'I think that bloody cat's hidden a dead thing under one of the sideboards' she sighed, 'and she won't let me have a look. I've not been in the first floor rooms since the last time she came out of hospital. You couldn't talk her into letting you take a peek, could you? She trusts you. And if you don't sort it out soon we'll end up with the environmental health 'round again.'

It felt treacherous nudging her towards an expedition to the junk room. She'd been waxing lyrical about Concorde's maiden flight. She'd been on it. There was champagne. 'I've still got a certificate somewhere upstairs,' she insisted. The double deadlock was nothing in comparison to the wall of stench we had to negotiate once the door was open. Oblivious, she sifted through piles of handwritten grocery receipts, scaled hillocks of obsolete electrical equipment and disembowelled suitcase after suitcase. There were little foil boxes winking at us from every flat surface.

'Are you planning to open a takeaway, Renie?'

'I just thought I'd put some of those dinners by for a rainy day. Waste not, want not.'

The last tin tray was balanced on a musty copy of The Forsyte Saga. She'd pressed a freesia from her wedding bouquet in the front cover.

Afterwards she insisted, sheepish, that there were no more scraps hidden in the stacks, but I could still smell something. I noticed it first when I answered a buzz from downstairs to find my old college sweetheart fidgeting on the step. He'd brought some post. He was sorry about the way things had just...well...come to a head. Yes, Jo was well. Moved to a flat around the corner, actually. Still drink in the Bullingdon on jazz nights. Be nice if we could still be friends. The faint aroma of leftovers billowed in with the thud of the door as it shut behind him. My gorge rose.

It was coming up from the tarmac with the heat haze, clinging more to some people than others. There was one chap, 'Walking Man,' we used to call him, who'd shuffle past the house cradling an enormous bundle of yellowing papers as though they were an orphaned child. He'd stop every few paces to tuck a stray sheet back into the swaddling. I came across him in Tesco, one day, humming gently amongst the special offers. I had to run. Lord knows how he ever managed to buy anything: a baby that big takes up both arms. If you can't even put it down to wipe its arse then it really starts to stink. In fact, the whole of Oxford reeked of the psychic nappies that no one could bear to change.

I kept all the doors and windows shut tight, but the smell seeped in through the cracks. I took hot showers, cold showers, used coal tar soap and salt scrubs. I stopped eating, but yesterday's dinners had already begun to ooze through my pores. As the odour concentrated, solidified, every movement met its resistance. The bookbinder asked me whether I was all right. Eventually, the strangers at the bus stop opposite plotted to kill me. Beckett started to make sense. 'Nervous exhaustion' the college doctor said, and benevolently signed me off for a fortnight, a month, two months...

And so it was that Prince Charming and I were married by mistake one frosty December afternoon. He'd promised me the clean, cool air of rural Gloucestershire. We barely said goodbye. I gulped down lungful after lungful of it, savouring the blank purity of each breath, and got better. It was the one promise he kept.

Renie sent us a pot of dried rose petals, and died a few months later. She'd been clambering over a long-defunct telly at 3am, in search of a summer vest she'd put by in 1978.

My Unsanitary Stalker
By Karen Jones

I wander down Sauchiehall Street, on my way to the Kelvingrove Art Galleries. It's a decent two mile stroll and it's never dull with so much going on around me.

I'm tempted by the smell of coffee from the half dozen generic outlets that mean this could be any city. I'm lured by the yeasty aroma from the bagel shops and 'sub' outlets that say this should really be an American city. I'm drawn to stop and watch the bizarre array of buskers: guy with a drum kit thrashing out a beat that means nothing to anyone but him; young guy playing bagpipes, badly; young woman playing violin, surprisingly well, and a Native American tribe playing traditional music.

I pass tracksuit clad, blinged and baseball-capped neds, speaking in that strange nasal whine, their girlfriends pushing Burberry prams, wittering 'hands free' into the latest mobile phones, their babies wearing dry-clean only bibs and sporting pierced ears at the age of two months. Classy.

In the doorways of every pub, every restaurant, every office block, storm clouds of smokers huddle, angry at the government's attempts to stop them committing slow suicide. I'm choking. There seem to be hundreds of them, everywhere, smoking two fags at a time and coughing phlegm all over the pavements. The air is cleaner in the pubs than it is outside since the smoking ban, though all those smells the smoke had hidden are fighting for prominence: stale beer, stale vomit and stale … well, I prefer not to dwell on what else is lurking.

Aye okay, it's not any city, it's Glasgow.

Not long now until I'll be cocooned in the fresh, cool air of the galleries. I walk a little faster, knowing the exercise does me good. Then it hits me; that noxious smell. And I know exactly what it is - who it is - that is destined to ruin my day. I don't even have to turn around. I can see his bald head, his fawn trousers and brown, suede bomber jacket. I know he's clutching a carrier bag and his chin is jutting out past his polo shirt collar, his feet clad in the oldest pair of trainers known to man. If I slow down and let him past I'll be stuck in his back-draft for the next mile.

This guy lives in the next village to mine. Everywhere I go, he appears. I have become convinced that he has me under satellite surveillance. Am I taking this too far? I don't think so. I leave the house to go for a run, there he is, marching towards me, his stench almost visible. I go to the local shops, he's just leaving and scores of people are clutching their stomachs and their noses, eyes wide in disbelief. I go into Glasgow, and he materialises behind me, which is always better than before me.

Until a couple of years ago, he lived with his mother, the smelliest woman on the earth. She always stank of stale urine and cooking fat, not a blend the perfume manufacturers are killing themselves to reproduce. She could clear entire streets. People would see her coming and rush to the nearest houses, begging for sanctuary. She must have spent her whole life thinking ours was the most deserted wee village in the world. When she died, local wags reckoned the morticians would give her the first wash she'd had in years, and they'd need a pressure hose.

And to her only son - to my stalker - she bequeathed the family stench. 'My time here is done now, son. I give you this foul odour and beseech thee: go forth and hum.'

And he has done her proud. I have this awful vision of him sitting on a sticky, stinky couch, eating yesterday's take-away curry, thinking,

'Hmm … really need to go for a pee, but I'll miss the next bit of Big Brother. Ach, I'll just do it here.' Then he sits, steam rising, drying out and enhancing the family heirloom.

Next day he goes out, but not until he's sure I'm running past, having to take great gulps of air to stop myself passing out from exertion.

For now, I speed up, desperately trying to out-run the waves of foul, unearthly odours that swirl around him. Sauchiehall Street looks like its playing host to some bizarre marathon, where the contestants are dressed in business suits or carrying shopping bags. We're all trying to escape. But I know there is no escape; he's everywhere. Him and his fawn trousers. Bet they used to be white.

One of these days I'll go out and breathe in fresh air. One of these days there'll be no sign of him. One of these days it'll be just me and my walk and my lovely day out.

Homecoming
By Jane Bratton

It's always perfect there at Ohio State University - ahem, THE Ohio State University - and today is no exception. My friend, Mike, and I trek to campus via I-70 to help our mutual niece move out of her dorm for the summer. It seems as if every time I visit my alma mater, a gentle rain falls before giving way to dog-day heat and humidity.

We decide to get off on the High Street exit and drive through downtown Columbus and its busy work-a-day world of pedestrians and compact cars and an occasional cyclist. The city blocks of the business district fade in the side-view mirrors as we make our way down High Street toward the poverty that is sandwiched between downtown and OSU. Boarded up buildings, tall grass and litter appear in stark contrast to the tidy downtown historic buildings that complement shiny, newer office towers behind us.

We roll down our windows and I soak in the scent of car exhaust fumes flirting with the early-June heat. Third Street. Fourth Street. Fresh tar covering pot-holes here and there melts under the mid-day sun, and I wallow in the smell of it, and the gas fumes, and I'm flashing back to my last trip to the local mechanic $380 ago.

We grab our niece and load her belongings into the car. We soon find ourselves on South campus, the gateway to THE Ohio State University. Traffic is slow so we have time to sight-see and reminisce. We decide to park the car and walk.

When you're a student at Ohio State, you learn to maneuver through alleys, past dumpsters and old, dirty mattresses. It is sometimes the quickest way to get from your off-campus apartment to your classes. We walk down Pearl Alley past broken bottles and garbage bins ripe with the putrid smell of trash, stale beer and an old man's piss. It rises, stinky

50

vapors, from the crumbling concrete until you feel like you're covered with it.

'It still smells the same,' I say to my niece. 'Some things will never change.'

We walk along Frat Row past the D-Zs and the Tri-Delts, trying to remember where Mike and I lived a few apartments away from each other (though we did not know each other then) more than twenty years ago. His former apartment building is worn but recognizable; mine has been torched and its innards gutted.

'If Claude's still the landlord,' I say, 'he'll renovate it into a three-bedroom apartment, you watch.

In five minutes we're on High Street, walking past bars old and new, and book stores and a tattoo parlor and McDonald's. The unmistakable stench of humanity greets us from sidewalks and sewer grates, and it presents itself with a familiarity that blends together to tell the weekend-tales of many in this Go Bucks! city: we drink, we puke, we eat, we puke again, we stumble home.

It's good to be back.

We decide to grab a gyro-lunch, and the hot, stagnant dining area is a perfect place for small talk over slices of lamb, sour cream and onions wrapped in warm shells. Our bellies full, we head back out onto High Street and down the stairwell to Bernie's.

I haven't been to Bernie's since 1985, when I treated myself to a toasted bagel and an imported beer after graduation rehearsal. Like everything else in Buckeye Nation, nothing really changes, it just gets older, like me and Mike and the bartender who brings us a beer and a shot, no charge.

The smell of this musty, damp basement, with its tapped kegs and nicotine-stained walls, cannot deny our history. Here where we used to watch bands play while drinking our beer and smoking our clove cigarettes. We were young then, wondering where our futures would take us. Little did we imagine the homecoming would be so memorable more than twenty years later.

Mike finds his name on the Beer Wall of Champions, circa 1987. 'Take a picture of me,' he says to our niece, pointing to his name on the plaque. 'Man, I sure worked hard for this.'

We finish our drinks and decide to head back to my sister's house. I light up a cigarette in this no-smoking city and extinguish it before I get in the car. After all, we can't take our niece back home smelling like she's just spent the afternoon in a bar with Uncle Mike and Aunt Jane.

Toxins make the world go 'round.

By Leslie Joseph

So I'm having this sort of epiphany, driving to work and entertaining a slight warmth between the proverbial (and literal, for that matter) legs. Don't shit where you eat. It's a crude saying, yes, and quite indicative of so many things I hate about the town I call home. Monroe is smallish, dramatic, and smelly on a number of levels.

My morning burn, in this case, is a result of thinking about the utter lack of physicality I am experiencing. I should be wearing an 'I Survived A Breakup And All I Got Was This Lousy Shirt' tee. As I automatically turn the curves that lead to my work, I ponder the possibilities for action. There has been no lack of offers, for sure. The problem is that nearly every one, save a very enthusiastic polyamorous pagan beer drinker, has involved people I've known for years. I feel like a landmark or a tourist attraction. I can hear them saying, 'Wow, we've come all this way; it would be a waste not to stop for a picture.' But as a little voice in my head keeps saying, 'Don't shit where you eat.'

That's kind of what my home town, Monroe, is like too. A gorgeous and historical riverfront is the main attraction for visitors. Antique district (read: a few streets that weren't busy doing anything else), downtown steadily being restored (read: gentrification), and a booming nightlife (you guessed it, we're a town of tired lushes) are just a few of the highlights. The money in Monroe, and of course you know there must be old money in a mid-size town on a riverfront, comes from vague sources. As one of the younger set, whom unlike many of my peers, didn't quite get around to debuting at the country club, I am still unsure as to where all the riches originated. The best clue I've had thus far is that the money is related to the stench in the air.

'Smells like money,' crow the old folks on humid days when the plumes from the paper mill are positively acrid. I can walk outside the front door of my work and watch the murky smoke rise. The breeze picks up, and a smell like carbonated sewage or burned plastic wafts my way. A few months back, my town made national news for a hazardous 'chicken waste product' spill on the interstate. People on the local news grimaced and drawled about the unbearable odor with which they had to cope as they drove home from work that afternoon. Automobile owners proclaimed that they'd had their cars washed professionally three times, and still the stench remained!

It was odd really, that no one seemed to correlate the chicken waste extravaganza with that 'money' odor that invades my nostrils every day. The paper mill that keeps our city in jobs emits an odor that is strangely close to the smell of the aforementioned offending chicken products. Maybe I'm just a whiney vegetarian. Maybe I'm a fascist recycling queen. Maybe my criminally high lack of ethnocentrism is finally rearing its ugly head. Who knows? I know that I watch droves of people enter the healthcare center where I work every day. 'Cancer' is a word like 'dog' or 'Christmas' around here. You can count on it. 'Cancer Alley' is to the south of me, luckily, but lately I've been thinking that the Northeast corner of the state where I live must be jealous of all that scandalous attention. We are doubling up on the emissions and the obscene amount of healthcare needed to deal with the fallout. It's as if no one here has ever truly heard of pollution or toxins and what these nasty words can do to people besides make them rich.

We love toxins! Toxins make the world go 'round. Monroe wouldn't exist if it weren't for toxins. Profits from peddling toxic drugs beef up the kids' allowances or pay for their various sundries through college. Toxins fill our veins as we medicate against the toxins that float in the dirty air that pays our bills that fund our community improvements that instill the toxic class warfare that creates the employees that punch the buttons on those wild machines that cloud up the air in the first place

Go toxins! It's brings me back to shitting where you eat. No one here will ever get much farther than recycling a can or two, because confronting the issue would mean tightening the purse strings. The ebb and flow of society will run like grooves in a record. The old guard will die and their semi-glamorous children will take over, young and spry until the 'money' in the air gets into their fresh lungs too. No one will shit where they eat, because they love eating. We wave our flags, we sponsor elementary school fund raisers, and we buy extra strong detergent because money is a really hard smell to get out of your dress clothes.

I'm trained not to shit where I eat, but the temptation is most times too delicious to resist. I struggle uphill so to speak, when I haul my metal, paper, and plastics to a local salvage company for voluntary recycling. I endure the strange stares when I wear my 'wage slavery' t-shirts to Wal-Mart, too tired and jonesing to work up an ethical dilemma over buying my organic bananas from the Devil. The Devil is so conveniently located and stays open much later than the Mom & Pop's. Mom and Pop need a little rest anyway, right?

All these thoughts have bulleted through my head on the ten minute drive to work; the smelly, head-ache inducing drive that leads, coincidentally, directly towards the money-scented mill about which I've mentally complained. I am watching the traffic light and halfheartedly calculating what my behaviors and thoughts mean. I shit where I eat when I recycle, when I boycott, and when I write protest letters to my senators and representatives. I don't want to pick up what my town is putting down.

This brings me back to my original quandary. I will work my long day and watch the plume of filth rise from the mill as I sit on the curb near my office to eat my lunch and get some 'fresh' air. Tonight I'll probably sit outside at a local pub and drink the beer that distracts me from the stench in the air. The oblivion on people's faces will be obvious as they reach into their $1000 purses or $400 pants pockets to pay for drinks. Should I slyly glance around the table and settle my eyes on someone who can alleviate my physical and mental discontent? Should I shit where I eat by taking the recreational plunge with the last few possibilities remaining in the little relationship ghetto I call home? If I shit where I eat this time, there won't be anyone to talk about it with afterwards. In a town like this, all you've got are the people with whom you commiserate about the gloom and doom. I am willing to go it alone when I recycle, when I bad-mouth my city's government, but it still remains unclear whose ideology I will choose after the charmingly noxious purple and orange sun sets on my town.

Tijuana Bouquet
By Lin Robinson

Like most cities, Tijuana has a smell all its own. Just more so. The third largest city in Mexico is located where there is no reason for a city to exist. Tijuana isn't where it is because of transportation hubs or natural resources or farmland: it exists because of an imaginary line. A political fiction that has slowly grown into a solid reality that's as visible as a scar from miles up in the sky. The border slices through the area like a fault line, lit up at night like mile after mile of ballparks: home team on defense, visitors have the ball. The California side is mostly an empty swath of cleared land or estuary; the Tijuana side tumbles right up to the fence in an ugly, haphazard sprawl. Sheared white sheep graze contently in the greener grass to the north, rough goats ramble in the chewed-down hills to the South.

A city built on the osmotic difference in legal status doesn't need belching furnaces and pungent factories: there's no harbor or railhead if they did build anything. The money has always been in tourism, with a high volume of people looking to drink, gamble, whore, divorce, score pills, shoot fireworks, see donkey shows, buy Cuban cigars, take cancer treatments, get switchblades, drive on beaches - the things they can't do back home. Then there are the assembly plants, putting together calculators and carburetors and keyboards and dolls from Japan or China to take advantage of American duty-free laws. And of course the lucrative traffic in narcotics and people who want to enter California illegally. To get the things they can't back home. Tijuana imports poverty and desperation from the South hoping to ship it North; it imports money and appetite from the North hoping to squeeze it dry. None of these industries makes much noise or smoke. But they have their own odors.

Walk through the metal turnstiles at the border and you notice the different odor immediately. First a waft of pure pollution: thirty two lanes of Interstate 5 crammed full of idling, overheating cars. Hundreds of waiting taxis, unencumbered by emissions standards. Big buses with no suspension slamming into potholes, wreathed in blue smoke.

Then you smell the food. It's hard to walk far in Mexico without smelling good food. Taco shops release an aerosol of carne asada grease, a tangy mist seeps out from chickens roasting on spits, sidewalk gyros flame aroma out of pork mixed with pineapple, intestines splatter in big iron woks, a smear of smoke transports the drip from young goats crucified over embers.

On the tourist strip along Avenida Constitución the location of odors becomes more specific. Tequila tasting here. Cuban cigars, amigo? Duty-free perfumes at Sara's. Cheaper perfume and a blend of spilt beer, sweat and point of purchase sex in front of Bambi's and Capricorn. Popcorn. Fresh tortillas coming off hot steel rollers. Massage oil. French rolls spilled out in bins. Chile peppers in hoppers. Herbs to impart health or potency. Onions, cilantro.

The Third World is only a few blocks beyond. Garbage burned in the open, raw sewage. Acrid tangs of curbside welding, fish offal, rotting vegetables, old clothes, used diapers, disinfectant. A blind man could find his way home through these pockmarked streets just by smelling the air. Which is what Eugenio had to do after the acid burned out his eyes, before he met Ronco. 'I thank God that it didn't take my nose and mouth or I would have lost my mind. Maybe I can't see or hear very well, but I can still taste and smell.' He holds up a hand, the skin like pork rind. 'I can still feel.'

As Eugenio moves, sipping tequila shots, lighting cigarettes for Ronco, I can see a shadow of his hand across the lower part of his face, normality against the lunar tissue above it. He had been fast, but not fast enough. If he'd gotten his hand up higher, he might have saved his vision, but lost his lips and nose. It's good these things happen so fast they save us from having to make conscious decisions like that

He reaches right to my pack of Faros on the table. He shakes one out and holds it up between two fingers, arm extended out to his side. Ronco leans to take it in between his lips. Eugenio picks up the lighter with the same sure movement, holds it firm against the corner of the table, flicks it. Ronco leans down for the light, puffs, blows on Eugenio's hand to let him know he can let the flame die. 'I smoked before,' Eugenio says, 'No longer. I need my nose these days. Just like I need this pendejo.' He and Ronco laugh mechanically: an old theme. 'But not as much as he needs me. The tarado can't even wipe his own ass.'

This appears to be literally true. Ronco has no hands. In fact, he has no arms. Or shoulders. His neck slopes down to his ribcage, giving him the configuration of a bowling pin. But he can see. Which allows this freakshow team to get around, Eugenio walking behind and to one side of the bulky Ronco, his hand always on his shoulder. They're inseparable, of course. You have to wonder what it would be like if they didn't get along so well. But then maybe they get along because they have no choice: circumstance determines our tastes more than we'd like to think. An old couple bound together by a bond stronger than pledges to the Church and State.

Their alliance allows them to live independently, except from each other. It's fascinating to watch Eugenio cooking with deft movements, Ronco leaning ponderously against the wall watching for trouble and mixing instructions and guidance with scatological byplay. There is nothing intimate or embarrassing about Eugenio putting clothes on Ronco or bathing him under the open pipe in their small cement block bath stall. How the ass-wiping works is going to have to remain a mystery. They move easily and naturally through the beaten paths of their life and job.

Because this peculiar symbiosis also allows them to make a living, such as it is. State lotteries are big business in Mexico. The poet Octavio Paz famously stated that Mexicans believe in nothing but the Virgin of Guadalupe and the National Lottery, as good a model as any of Mexico's uneasy balance between God and Government. All ticket sales are controlled by the administration, which gives preference to the crippled, infirm, psychologically unstable and otherwise unemployable. One result of that is a cantina located between the dingy lottery office, with its layers of political exhortation peeling off the walls, and the 'Revu' strip where passers-by comprise a major cash herd. The bar is called 'Nights in July' for some reason, but could just as easily be 'Fantasia by Bosch'.

60

This is the watering hole and professional conference hall for the Tijuana chapter of the wretched of the earth. Those who can walk around and make change, at least.

With a smell all its own, also. Men with crutches and epilepsy and hooks for hands spill a lot more, so the odor of stale habanera and tequila is stronger inside. Some of the ticket hawkers here are incontinent at times, and anyway there is always somebody getting confused and pissing on the wall. So there's that note in the gumbo of smells, as well as the cheapest tobacco, the least fastidious whores, the weakest marijuana, and the deep-fried chicken necks that tend to go bad before they sell. But Eugenio will tell you about the intangibles. 'It's the odor of vale madre,' he says seriously.

An extremely Mexican phrase that's not about mothers but about not giving a good rat's ass. An attitude that does seem to run rife in the place: it's a raucous, milling swarm of disfigured, dysfunctional locos with that slight hysteria of men drinking themselves to death to keep from doing something worse and laughing too loud so they won't feel something even scarier than that.

'You can smell it on a man,' Eugenio says while Ronco, as always, solemnly nods to back up his every pronouncement. 'I can't really describe it. It's like fear. You know the odor at once, but what would you say about it?' I trade nods with Ronco. Fear is an influential part of Tijuana's olfactory make up. Three weeks before, working on a story about illegal border crossings, I was brought into a small bedroom so packed with Guatemalan peasants that they all had to sit with their knees up to fit inside. One look at the big white guy in khaki pants and the fear pressed out of their pores like a gust of panicked pheromones blasting out the doorway - acrid, with notes of straw and nitric acid. Eugenio is right: what can you say about it?

The pair are among the top earners among lottery pimps. Ronco steams through crowds, the tractor of the enterprise, Eugenio trailing him with the tickets slung over one shoulder, spieling the Big Chance, wheedling the marks to have the balls for a shot at the Fat One, making change with the sure-handed dexterity of the sighted. Ronco keeping an eye on the color of the folding money.

There's a rumor Ronco's arms were hacked off by the same narco enforcer that blinded Eugenio, but there is nothing to it. Ronco was an enforcer: he messed up, so they chopped off his hands at the elbows and infection took care of the rest. Typical TJ tale. Eugenio was a hustler, weaseling in on deals. But he was also a dapper ladies man who weaseled in on the wrong lady. Both had a hard time of it before they ran into each other and hooked up.

There's also a rumor that the two of them killed the man who threw the acid in Eugenio's face. A rumor that Eugenio confirms. Ronco saw him staggering out of a bar in the Zona Roja, alone. He hurried to follow the guy down the block and into the parking lot behind the Alaska Motel, dragging Eugenio along. He stopped at a taco stand and demanded that the taquero loan them his knife.

They caught up to the guy fumbling for his car keys. Ronco steamed up and kicked him into the car door. He kicked his legs out from under him and started yelling instructions to Eugenio. The narco flopped on the ground, fighting the liquor, kept off balance by Ronco's mulekicks. Eugenio moved in on him, scything with the knife. The guy must have a good look at the face he had ravaged before he got to his feet. Where Eugenio sliced through his stomach his entrails spilled out all over his belly and thighs.

'He stopped cutting. He know the cabrón had it then,' Ronco says. Eugenio nods modestly. Not that difficult for a man of his gifts. 'It was the smell. I'm telling you, there is nothing like it. If we think, we know our guts are full of food and shit. But there's all this other stuff in there, too. Smells you never see anywhere else. Disgusting.' Ronco nods emphatically. Yeah, sickening smells.

'I was about to come in my pants from getting the revancha on that guy. But the smell almost made me throw up,' Eugenio goes on. 'All these dark green, slimy stinks. And you know, fart. Like all his farts coming out at once. Bad ones. Piss kind of smells that make your eyes water. And fear. And then another one. Death. It's just like a gasp of this thin, gray odor. And you know he's dead.'

Ronco makes a grunt that causes Eugenio to reach for a Faro and hold it up for him, then strike the lighter. He sets it down and shrugs. 'It was the kind of smell, you know, a real Tijuana kind of smell.'

La Muerta
By Rachelle Hafen

'The funny thing is that death is actually feminine in the Spanish language,' said Hector. Hector looks like a Santa Claus, and he doesn't look Hispanic, but his accent gives him away. Especially when he is speaking Spanish.

Megan didn't think it was very funny. The tequila was making her eyes water just from the aroma. She didn't know why she was at the Cabaret Electric event either. She had been invited by the musical act to recite poetry, and since it was a friend trying to raise awareness, Megan was there. She wasn't listening. She was drinking tequila and Lev with Hector the Mexican Santa.

Hector excused himself so Megan turned her attention back to the bartender. He was cute, in a very approachable, almost codependent, way. She was in the middle of a long verbal gush about the musicians when Hector interrupted her.

'You are next Mija!' He was very excited to see her performance. She had confessed to him outside, when the sun was setting, that she was an actress not a poet. He had informed her that it didn't matter, and that she was the only woman there, maybe even the first. The place smelled like new paint.

Now standing in front of the other artists she began to understand the point of it all. There was no audience this time. Just an open forum of artists, for artists. With a few self-deprecating jokes about the poems, she read to her remaining peers.

Going on last has its tipping point. It is easy by then to act as you wish because there is no time to hesitate. However, once the event winds down and the adrenaline wears off, you find yourself drunk. Drunk, and with little money. You might have even spent it on tequila shots for Hector. Alcohol must have a stronger scent than fear.

'You're only a bambina, too young to buy an old man a drink.' Hector had offered.

'Please don't insult my talents,' she replied with a sneer, jarring a laugh from his beer-rippled belly.

But now the art was finished and they had to leave the parking lot before the cops noticed them. She would look like a hooker, hanging around such a drunken old man. He seemed to feel the same way, so he offered her the wheel to the car. Hookers do not typically drive, after all.

Megan had always been a sucker for opportunism. Here she was driving a perfectly decent car with the 'new' scented tree hanging from its rearview mirror. Here on the wrong side of town the cabs make a point to be very tardy, in case you are too drunk to pay. They seem to think the drunks just wander off eventually.

She was grateful for this stretch and to be in the driver's seat. Her last twenty bucks was still stashed in her stinky tennis shoe. Megan had a reputation for losing things when tequila was involved, and money smells like sweat either way.

Making small talk with Hector was easy. Megan's Spanish was limited so when he started inviting her on a future play-date, it was relatively easy to describe her 'crazy boyfriend' and his jealousy. When they got to the boyfriend's house, it was even easier to keep him from following her in. Megan's boyfriend is part Mexican and goes by Pico. For one Chicano to another, Hector obliged.

'Wait my angel,' he said as she parked.

'What for, Senor?' She was tired now

'Where should I piss?' He gestured to the houses.

'Please use the gutter,' was her best idea.

She was watching his cover, with her back to him, clutching her skateboard firmly with her left hand and shuffling her feet as quietly as possible. Megan was beginning to feel as if something was on the cusp of occurring. Maybe it was the smell of moisture in the dry desert air.

'My angel, would you like some peyote?' Hector was naughty for a Santa. The barn door on his jeans was forgotten and unzipped. He was standing next to the driver side door.

'Yes.' Funny that she didn't need to question herself.

He reached into his pocket and pulled out a cellophane bag. It looked like the cover of a cigarette pack. He reached in and grabbed a pinch and she instinctively opened her mouth. He sprinkled some dust down her throat.

'It is for praying.' He looked in her eyes for the first time.

'That's what I've heard.' She didn't know what else to say. This so-called-peyote happened to smell and look just like sage.

Megan left Hector quickly after that, since she felt nervous and stupid. It was a good thing Pico was up waiting for her, because as she approached his front door she heard Santa leave and she knew it would be a long time, if ever, that she saw him again.

As usual, Pico did not ask her many questions. When she told him about the peyote, his eyes were the size of saucers.

'Do you have any drugs left?' is what he said.

'Open your mouth angel, it's time to pray.' she answered.

Magnets

By Sarah Rose Etter

It is early in the morning and I am in a taxi cab. There is a man driving the yellow car and he is foreign. He smells. I cannot place the smell exactly: phantom cigarettes, spices, and flatulence. The cab smells like weeks of sleep in the same bed. It smells like dirty sheets.

'Where can I take you?'

'Mass General' I tell him, and then I look out the window as if I have not seen the city before, I am pretending that the buildings are beautiful and new. But everything is really covered in ice and salt. I am watching the people on the sidewalks and I secretly hope that one of them slips on the ice, takes a real fall, something slapstick and hilarious. But nobody falls.

I have a suspicion that the smelly man took the long way round. I don't know the area well enough to curse at him and so I pay him seven dollars and then stand in front of the hospital, quietly, as if it is a church. The hospital is a tall glass building, and there are ambulances everywhere. Some have blaring sirens and others sit quietly, waiting for the next old woman to pick up the phone about her husband's faulty lungs, heart or liver.

The front doors are made of the clean kind of glass. I wonder who cleans these doors. I imagine an older woman cleaning them every hour on the hour. That's how clean the glass is.

Inside, the white floors and soft shoes upset me, miniature implications that everyone should just remain calm. There is a desk with the word HELP strung up above it. A woman sits at the desk wearing coordinating jewelry. She smiles at me

'What can I help you with today, dear?'

68

Her smile is so wide, so big; it is as if she is making up for the bad news that I have not heard yet. It is pre-pity.

'I need to find 225 Ellison,' I am saying, as if I am another girl who is calm and not yelling loudly on the inside. There is a roaring lion perched inside of my left ear. It feels like vertigo.

'Just take a left and use the E elevator,' she says too kindly. She has a fluorescent smile and I see it again.

In the silver elevator, I stand next to a man on a gurney and a black man dressed in scrubs. The man on the gurney is covered in clear tubes and he smiles at me. I can see the pity oozing out of his mouth. I smile back a bigger smile because I pity him more. This is how it goes here. It is like bartering.

When I get to the second floor, I find room 225. A man with a gentle voice quietly asks me to fill out paperwork and change into a hospital gown.

My handwriting is very sloppy as I fill in my name, bra size and history. I check little boxes to let everyone know that I am not lactating or menstruating and that I do not have any metal rods in my head. I date and sign the white sheets. The man with the gentle voice takes me to a small room. He hands me the gown.

I take off my silver ring and slide the earrings out of my ear. If I do not take out the metal, the MRI machine will rip it out of my body at a horrible angle. The jewelry will rip through me like gunshots from inside. That's what the doctor said. He said once there was a man who had a sliver of a bullet left in his knee after he had been shot. Years later, when he got an MRI, the machine tugged the metal out of him and he was shot again, from inside out.

I take off my t-shirt, sweatshirt, bra and jeans. I fold each article of clothing into a perfect square and stack them neatly as I remove them, as if by being tidy I will be spared all of the cancer, tumors, and cysts they will find beneath my skin. I slide a faded blue hospital gown against my skin. There are two ties in the front that I knot together.

I sit in a chair and wait for the Spanish nurse to call me in. I look down at the gown and wonder if anyone has died in it, or if those gowns get thrown away. I imagine it saves a lot of money to reuse them, but it just seems unethical to make patients wear hospital gowns that have clothed a dead body.

The Spanish nurse surprises me. She is nice, but besides that she is wielding a large needle. I wasn't expecting this and so I turn my head when she slides the silver into my arm, a prick that I must take a deep breath for.

'All done!' the Spanish nurse says cheerfully.

I look down at my arm and see pieces of colored plastic hanging against my skin.

'What the hell is this?' I ask her.

'Oh, that's for the IV.'

'What IV?'

'We have to put the contrast in.'

'The contrast?'

'Well, we're going to inject you with the contrast so we can see your breasts better on the machine.'

'Oh.' And the tears are pushing at me now. I do not know how to be an adult at all of these hospitals, these death Meccas. I want my mother here, so she can explain all of the terminology and technicalities.

I look at the temporary needle in my arm and I begin frantically thinking of my funeral and what they will find left over in my bureau drawers when I am dead. I wonder what they will think of all the things I have kept, the bits and pieces of life, when I'm gone.

In the background, the doctors and nurses argue over body parts.

'Do you want to check out a breast or a liver?' says a doctor.

'I'm sick of doing breasts, you do the breast,' says the nurse.

'You always get the livers.'

'If I have to look at one more breast today, I'm out of here.'

'Let's flip a coin over it,' the doctor says and they both laugh. I do not think they are funny.

Another nurse comes to get me; another sympathetic face. She takes me into a room and above the door is a sign that says 'X-Ray in progress'. It is like a recording studio. In the room, there are needles, sinks, pieces of machinery and trashcans for medical waste. In the center of the room there is a big beige tube with a table that slides in and out. The table has two holes cut out for my breasts.

'Just take off your robe and lay down on your stomach,' the new nurse says, while the Spanish nurse unfolds a screen to place in front of a giant window in the room.

'We don't want any peeping Toms, now do we?' she says.

I smile at her faintly and do as I'm told. I lie down on the table, my breasts filling the two holes and then hanging in the air while I shiver against the chill of the machine.

The new nurse slips a black rubber ball into my hand that is connected to a wire.

'This is your panic button,' the nurse says. 'If the contrast makes you sick or you get claustrophobic, just press this and we'll get you right out.'

I rest my head on the pillow between my arms as the Spanish nurse slips the contrast needle into my IV and presses it.

'The contrast is going to feel cold in your veins,' the new nurse warns. 'But that's totally normal. If you feel your throat start to swell up, then just hit the panic button. That only happens to one in one hundred thousand people, so you should be fine.'

The nurses press a button and the table with the holes for my breasts slides back into the beige tube. The IV jumps inside of my skin as the contrast is injected into my veins. All around the needle, I can feel a slight burn and then my veins feel chilled, cool, from the inside out.

Then there is a succession of loud clicks, and then a whirring sound that is piercing. On the microphone, the nurses say soothing things that pipe into the room where I am surrounded by a giant whirring magnet. They say 'It's just a little while longer, Sarah' and it sounds patronizing. I want to fight them.

There is a metallic taste in my throat, a cool silver taste, the contrast coating the back of my throat. The snaps keep coming at quicker and quicker intervals, and the soothing voices hush 'Be very still, Sarah. Be very still.'

I think about the glamour shots being done of my tits. I wonder why we haven't made room for a feather boa, maybe some glitter, a little bit of pressed powder.

Then I think about the lines they will draw beneath my breasts and then the scalpel. I think about the blood that will slide out from my skin, and how the doctors will not care because they are used to all of that liquid red. I think about my ribs wrapped in white bandages, about weeks of vomiting, about the removal of the evil things. Part of me wants to be cut. The other part wants to go to Mexico where the doctors' secretary can't call my cell phone and I won't have to hear her voice lilting with reminders about how they just don't know anything for certain.

When the magnet is done, the nurses pull the needle out of my veins and I feel woozy as they show me the door.

'Can I see the pictures?' I ask the Spanish nurse. I want to see what the insides of my breasts look like, my ribs and my boobs electric-shocked into black and white frames. I wonder if I could maybe see my heart, if the magnet was strong enough.

'No,' she says. 'You can't.'

And in the back of my mind, I just hope she finds cancer. I want them to cut me open and remove the worst parts. I hope that my MRI screens are illuminated on a white board and that a giant black tumor blots out most of the picture, an ink blot under my skin. I hope that my veins and tissue, glowing like Las Vegas billboards, show them how nasty I am inside.

I think about the cancer as a slow friend creeping through me. Maybe it has already conquered my breasts and has moved on to other things. Perhaps my lungs and lymph nodes have joined in on the party. I think about the way the scalpel will feel. I think about the thin, precise line of blood it will leave behind. I think about the months of not working, about the chemotherapy dropping weight from my body, about becoming bald.

And by the time I am outside, by the time I have walked back through the clear glass, I have convinced myself that cancer might not be so bad after all.

Poetry

A Modern Heartsong

By Symonne Torpy

The grey bird took wing
She used to be a dove
Her call once sweet
Had been devoured by unknown prey.
Metallic carnivores
Chattering to each other
Grind, clatter and roar
The heart song of a modern age.

A bakery on Oxford St.
Heat from clever pastries
Rising in the cool of the morning.
Breathe in the aromas
Of asphalt sweating in the afternoon
Billowing clouds
Of noxious gas
Swallows singing; cell phones ringing

Walking barefoot down Paddington
The prick of a needle
Screaming sensation
And the stench of old bourbon

A woody perfume
Oaks spreading their limbs
Toward the sky
The smell of drying woodchip
Make way for roads

What are trees anyway?
Sky scrapers stretching strong limbs
Towards the building line

Chanel, Gucci and Ralph Lauren
Clinging to the jackets
Of driven women
And their men
The clicketty clack of heels

The pulse of a city
Respirating as one.

Bangla Town

By Jewels Johnson

Shoreditch
stitched
with wannabes
Spitalfields
unpeeled
overloaded
with bric a brac
a well travelled man
sells treasures from a sack
and amidst the nick nacks
tells me my tale.
It unravels, his face
an old screwed up tea bag
and I'm hung out to dry.
Unveiled
and stale odour clings to me
a days worth of fags.
Jack the Ripper once haunted these alleys
etching up notches of each whore;
now people just come here to score.
But I'm wandering into
my paradise, my oasis.
Here, I am faceless.
Nothing superficial here,
gold elephants decorate the arcs
that I pass beneath
and I suddenly realise

that I can breathe
here,
leave everything behind,
soak in sunsets, saris, silks and scents
of spicy jewelled
precious seasoning.
I believe in this,
this kiss
of life,
I want it:
this bliss.
Bangla men welcome me in to be intoxicated
by their tastes
I am already enchanted, bewitched,
voices wail sounding holy and sacred
they fall through me like a sigh.
This wandering vagrant
Bangla Town is a strange exotic fruit
rising through me and taking up root.
Bare foot I walk with dry, scaled lizard feet,
I seep up the history of the Jews who once walked these streets.
Where the aroma of soup kitchens was so heady with perfume
it made buildings from the smoke shapes,
rooms escaped from the chimney stacks.
I wander down into Brick Lane,
this place runs through my veins
my heart does not beat in my chest
it's obsolete.
But here in Brick Lane
where I delete
all bad memories erased
my finger tips trace
walls that whisper
and I'm a good listener
Strains of Amy Winehouse
her melancholy refrain

the perfect sountrack
to bottle up my pain.
Across the city
billows of smoke smudge
a pink moon
smothering the skyline
like greedy vines.
For the moment the city, it crowns
Because Camden Town is burning down.

In the City as a Child
By Charlotte Scadeng

Back to the street where I lived
In the city as a child
The estate filled with bashed in cars,
Dog shit on the grass.

Sun filled Saturdays playing BMX Bandits
Round blocks of flats.
Sunday roasts wafting from windows
As I sit on the dead lawn in summer.

Mum shouts out the window
And I run into the piss-infested stairwell,
Drunks on the steps, drooling, swearing
As I skip past, oblivious to adulthood.

The best days spent playing in the roads
Car fumes blocking my asthmatic lungs
Roller skate Sundays. Penny chews,
Strawberry shortcakes mixed with smog.

Innocent imaginings, games and adventures
On garage roofs.
Rope swings, dens and muddy knees
Mixed with all my city smells.

City smells
By Nii Amu Swaniker

Rainwater falls slate, the acidic underlay thick.
Dank dampness, the smell of filth and carelessness, an insult of scent.

Uniformed figures, wax-like, expressionless.
Sharp nicotine and roasting, smoked coffee inject life to minds of deadline and haste.
I'm alive.

A faint slither of sweat, bodies pressed, the rusty heat of claustrophobia. Madness ensues.

The air vents breathe noxious warmth through suffocating stabs of carbon and exhaust. Forgotten waste fetid with cloying decay.

Noise and chaos. The nasal sting of heated metal and abuse of pollution. I retreat.
The way unclear and awareness heightened.

A transient cacophony of spices: nutmeg and burnt pepper, sweet and biting lights the senses and ignites the hunger. I follow through.

My mind heavy, the sun lights the streets.

Cloudless
By Leslie Joseph

Your city smells like ginger.
That bed we slept in smelled
like hay. If I go far enough
away, there is a place
where no one knows what it's like
to eat blueberries
straight off the bush.
The scent of your skin
will fade from my memory
like an old sachet
whose bouquet has become
impossible to decipher.

Crandall Canyon
By Alicia Hoffman

'Hope is in order at this point. Heavy doses of hope'
 - Utah Gov. Jon Hunstman August 8, 2007

Tonight, the starlight drips hope slowly
onto the sidewalks and the lamp posts,

the downtown lofts and the offices
of ghosts, the cemetery beyond

the highway is still as the puddles pooling
into small lakes on the garden and the lawn.

Tonight, it is almost as if this entire city
could find them alive, blackened with the smog

of their own boxed metropolis, as if the silent
smell in the air is a prayer that has gained

the weight it needs to travel from far below
that mountain in Utah. Tonight, the air

in this city is the scent of coal and ash, sulphur
and mineral, it is the still wind of elements, iron

rich and fertile. In this air, it is possible
to believe we can push easily into that cave, past

our own monolithic skyscrapers, the stalagmites
of civilization, and brush the metallic sheen

of sky. I wonder what they are saying,
if they are still alive. I wonder if they are

singing, or weeping, or calling out apologies
to forgetful gods. I would like to think

they are sleeping, that they are dreaming
sensational dreams of their own cities,

that they are studying the maps of the sites
most sacred to them, searching out what should be

saved, what it is they have always wanted to see,
what they would most like to remember, the lines

of the roads leading to what is most important, that
invisible municipality, the scent that beckons home.

Midtown on Blutgasse
By Rachel Lisi

Seize the scent of what the moon has left behind
on the aerials of the building
on the eyelids of the dreamer
in the reflection of the window
on the stains of our lips on the sheet on the pillow.

When the dawn comes smell melon pink flesh
and cucumber green air in the large open eye.
Streets strong with exhaust, electricity, coffee and sound scrapes.
The woman next to us on the bus sweat pungent with wolf sex.
It must have been hard because she's over-ripe and sweet,

like the banana in the old man's left pocket.
We pass him on Blood Lane on the click and the crack
where periwinkle whores smoke ginger cigarettes
where a heated breeze on the back of a sun whip
whispers to a mangle of sour fur called alley cat doing hard time.

Holding his hands out they look like a bird taking flight
and are redolent of nickel and copper
and the coal he mined fifty-three years ago when
we were left floating in the black movements
of star shadow and the milky soup of nothing.

We'll never notice as we walk down into our day
into the red might of the stoplight
into the misplaced memory of mother's perfume

the spice of his open fingers carries us back
to a time we stood close to our father.

No Hot Ashes
By Dan Beck

Like burnt pork ends,
the 4AM summer creeping
of the city crematoriums
thick smoked stench,
crawls across moistened,
dew speckled skin.

Tobacco blackened lungs
demand a fix,
whisky from a brown bag
to hot lips.

The lingering rot
of vomit from
some hour I'll
never recall.

I'm drunk...

... this bench is wet.

No One Smokes Here Anymore
By Adam "Bucho" Rodenberger

No one smokes here anymore
but the walls still cough
from aftershock and grime,
time colored on the paneling
in swirls of cancered scribblings,
perfumed phero-moans,
and pints of imports
spilled into the crevices,
a bath of funk-sin functioning
as faux wallpaper.

No one smokes here anymore,
they step out into dusk,
puff-puffing at the passerby
and flicking butt to curb,
quick-soaked up in puddles
of last night's arid lightning play,
emanating cloy and backbone
over waste thrown out that day
from unfinished five-star lunches
and fast food wrappers
hastily McLittered away.

No one smokes here anymore,
they've all grown up and quit,
tired of twice-washing good shirts
just to sniff clean

amidst crowds
of the hair sprayed and over-cologned.
No one smokes here anymore
but the walls still cough
in smoke rings
of near forgotten
anecdotes.

Spearmint Dust
By Caroline Dotson

Appearing before her
the smoke stacks rise.
Steamed iron burning reeks
against a hot dry sky.

Walking downtown she looks
in windows of the shops.
Smelling spearmint dust behind
gum chewing smacks.

Sitting on the porch.
Her back to a field of sage.
The scent of musty rain
filling the cupped petals.

The flowers
in pots.

Sunflowers (after William Blake)

James Meredith

A young woman boards the metro
& takes the seat beside me.
She is tall, fair, pretty, smells
of cigarettes & Sunflowers,
the perfume that you used to
wear when we first met, the scent
which used to catch the breath
in my throat & set off a
warm tumbling
inside of me.

It was your everyday perfume
you told me. You'd picked it up
cheap in Boots.
You wore more expensive scents
on nights out or on special
occasions – something with a touch
of class.

But it's the Sunflowers I remember.

I turn my face to the window
as the bus moves slowly through town.
Out in the street the wind blows;
the skirts of women flap like flags
in the breeze. Builders huddle in
the half-built shell of an

office block, their palms cupped
protectively around cigarettes, taking
a break from making Belfast whole again.

I close my eyes & breathe deeply the scent
of Sunflowers as I wait for
this travellers journey to be done.

This City Smells
By Graeme Sandford

This city smells of many things
Abuse, neglect, decay.
Its streets are full of folded wings
That refuse to fly away.

Broken, forgotten promises litter the way
Decomposing where they fell
Giving off the pleasant bouquet
Of a stagnant wishing well.

The air is composed of gas and lies
Which we breathe in as we labour
The taste of truth is hard to find, defies
Our brittle buds to savour.

The rivers run and teem with life,
All distasteful and alarming,
The corrupted taint of wrong is rife,
Our water supplies self-harming.

Nothing grows upon the land,
Except sores that spread and ooze,
And pus-like smells upon your hand,
stains of vomit, concoctions banned, blood and bile and booze.

This city smells of many things,
As it swings from a hangman's rope,
Foetid lives, tired, cancerous springs,
But mostly of old, discarded hope.

Stories

Smell a Rat

By Chris Lee Ramsden

The original recording:

Flynn sat down heavily, clutching the mobile phone to his chest. The office was full of people and he was relieved that nobody had noticed his entry.

'What you got there, Flynn?' said Angus, his friend, colleague and confidant.

Flynn waved him off.

'Nothing,' he said, and tugged at a tangle of wires sticking out of a half open desk drawer. A shower of pens and paper clips hit the floor.

He fumbled a set of headphones into his ears and plugged the other end into the mobile phone. It felt greasy to the touch, and gave off a vile odour – something like old cheese. Good thing he didn't need to use it to make a call: he wouldn't want to hold that under his nose. He hit play.

A click. A cough.

'Detective Constable Lee investigating. Dropping interrogation of Giles St John Gower. Old tosser knows something, but isn't letting on.'

The voice was low. He must have been holding the phone tight to his cheek, with the mouthpiece almost pressed to his lips. His breathing was close, excited.

'Screaming from above, sounds female. Must be in the attic, I'm going up.

'Am now climbing a narrow staircase. Each step is worn down to a U-shape. Not easy to keep my footing. Can't see old St John Gower making it up h –

'Fuck the judge!'

Flynn resisted the urge to rip out the earphones. Detective Constable Lee must have dropped his phone.

Now the screaming was clear, and was punctuated by a second person's groans.

'Think I've twisted something. Using my hands to pull myself up the last... few... steps.

'Attic. Lots of wooden panelling. I can smell the age of this place. The dust must be hundreds of years old. Centuries of dried skin and woodworm. And there's something else. Solvents? Varnish?

'Screaming's stopped. I have a visual. Female Caucasian endomorph, standing in the doorway. She has her back to me. And a hand over her mouth.

'Established visual contact. It's Sarah. I spoke to her this morning. She's a witness – the last person to see him. Sarah Greenway. Spoke to her already. This morning.

'And now she's making repetitive jabs with her left index finger. Can't see round her fat... but there's something in the room. Something dangling from the ceiling. Whoa, she's turned, and is heading this w – '

The recording broke down into a farrago of distorted screams and dull thuds.

'Christ. My leg –

'Witness Greenway spiked my leg with her fucking heels. Lost visual. She's tumbled past me down the stairs.'

Flynn could just make out a string of shrill expletives.

'Sounds like she's OK.

'Shi-ite.

'Sorry. Unable to get up. I might've broken something. Not much feeling in my legs.

'Am now crawling to the door using arms only. Ugh, put my hand in something sticky. There's lots of it all over the floor. Smells like... nothing really. Can't detect any smell over the dust and age of this place. It is, though, slightly viscous. Carrying out quick ad hoc analysis of texture and taste – '

Detective Constable Lee's violent retching filled Flynn's ears in glorious stereo. And it dawned on Flynn what he'd smelt on the phone. Vomit. And whatever that viscous fluid was.

'Semen. Human semen.'

Flynn's stomach lurched. He dropped the phone into his lap.

'And, now I've tainted the evidence. Not much chance of forensics getting a good DNA sample, I'm afraid. Unless they can separate semen and sick. And blood. That's my blood, I think.

'Now I see him. Hanging from the rafters. By his tie. Moving in to get a definite ID.

'There are two identical plastic bags at his feet. Common to high street retail outlets, specifically Marks & Spencer. The first – '

Rustling.

' – contains three large Israeli oranges and six 'Pyjama' bananas. From Fiji. There's evidence to suggest a seventh banana has been removed. The banana was torn free. The sap of the exposed stalk is still tacky. Suggests the banana was removed recently, local weather conditions, humidity and ripeness of banana notwithstanding.

'The second plastic bag has been placed over subject's head. Now removing second plastic bag.

'It's him. I'm sure of it.

'A fourth orange – large, Israeli – is lodged in his mouth.

'It's an enormous. Fucking. Orange. Lips white and taut and fuck me cracked and torn at the corners like a Chelsea smile.'

A series of clicks suggested the tape recorder had been paused and restarted several times. More vomiting?

'Searching subject's inside jacket pocket. I've got his wallet. ID confirmed as the Right Honourable Reginald Harding M.P. And what's this?

'Oh Reggie.'

Pause. Nothing but breathing.

'Further investigation reveals semen coagulated at tip of exposed penis. Trousers and underwear – lacy, lady's, M&S – are snagged around subject's ankles, which are...'

A sound like a sword being drawn from a scabbard.

'...fourteen centimetres above the attic floorboards. And fucking semen.'

Rubbing, rummaging.

'Time of death estimated at fourteen hundred hours. Cause of death: asphyxiation –

'Jesus fucking Christ. He's rammed a banana – the missing seventh banana – up his arse. Only the tip sticking out. Explains the flood of semen – must have ruptured his prostate.'

Flynn hit pause. He looked up and caught Angus' eye.

'You'd need a stone banana,' he said.

'Stone banana?' Angus said.

It was no good. Flynn pulled out his earphones.

'It's from Gower. He told me to listen before we brief the others. The muppet the police sent over recorded it all on his mobile, blow by blow.'

'You're kidding.' Angus scrambled over. 'And what's with the stone banana?'

'You've no idea. Listen to this.'

Flynn pulled out the headphones and hit play. Detective Constable Lee's voice sounded tinny and distant.

'… pints of semen. Bananas. Big fucking Oranges. So big I can't even get one in my m –'

'Let me help you,' a second voice said, also close.

'Jesus,' Angus said. They listened to several seconds of Detective Constable Lee's muffled grunting. And a second person breathing hard.

'There's someone in there with him.'

The grunts stopped and there was a couple of dull thuds.

'Body hitting floor?'

And a very close-up clatter.

'Sounds like he dropped his phone,' said Angus.

Footsteps grew louder in the tinny speaker.

'Someone's picked it up.'

The two men stared at the phone in Flynn's lap, listening to recorded silence, engulfed in the odour of necrotic bodily fluids.

*

The Six O'clock News Eulogy
[Switch to Camera Three]

And on a more subdued note, Tory backbencher and celebrated right-wing provocateur Reginald Harding M.P. died peacefully in his bed last night. Renowned for championing country sports,

[Cut to clip of foxhunter in full regalia mounted on a white stallion using the bell-end of a brass hunting horn to beat off anorak-clad protesters]

particularly foxhunting,

[Cut to close-up of elegant leather riding boot, released from stirrup, swinging into protester's alarmed face]

his health had been in steady decline since, and I quote, 'This barbaric ban on the sport of gentlemen – English gentlemen to boot.'
    The Prime Minister led a minute of silence in the House of Commons earlier today and, in the eulogy that followed, declared the Right Honourable gentleman would be sorely missed.

[Switch to Camera One]

And finally today, from grizzly to teddy – have you ever wondered how one of the most dangerous animals in the Northern Hemisphere became the teddy bear in every child's pram? A new exhibition at the Natural History Museum aims to shed some light on...

*

What the Papers Said:

DETECTIVE'S DEMISE DEFIES DECENCY

Yesterday, Detective Constable Christopher Lee was found dead in an attic above the House of Commons still clutching a shopping bag full of fresh grapefruit, pears and apricots. Despite suspected attempts by the London Metropolitan Police Force to mount a cover-up, our reporters were able to obtain firsthand witness accounts of the mysterious circumstances surrounding Detective Constable Lee's demise.

The detective's body was discovered in the attic earlier this afternoon by the deputy assistant P.A. to the Minister of Transport, Sarah Greenway. Alerted by her screams, the Right Honourable Giles St John Gower M.P. rushed up three flights of stairs to her assistance. Despite her traumatic experience, she's said to be comfortable and will soon be able to help police with their inquiries.

Hero of the hour, Mr St John Gower, said, 'The body was surrounded by, and covered in, vomit and semen and there was a large piece of fruit in its mouth and a plastic bag over its head.

'He'd been sniffing around earlier on, asking questions and talking to himself. We must count ourselves fortunate that the Detective Constable's sexual experimentation was limited to groceries, and that there were absolutely no children, animals or Members of Parliament involved whatsoever.'

Forensic scientists at Scotland Yard have been unable to verify the ownership of the various bodily fluids found along with the body. 'It wouldn't be too difficult to isolate the fluids and get DNA samples,' one forensic assistant remarked, 'But we just haven't been allocated the resources on this one.'

The case is due to be heard in court later this week where the coroner is expected to pass a verdict of 'Death by Misadventure'.

Spoiled
By Kelly Smith

They left the pub knowing exactly where it would lead, stepping away from the pounding bass beats into the bitter night air, without words, both wanting each other for this night, stripping away the pretence, away from the endless small talk and false-fixed smiles. He lit the tip of his cigarette and threw away the match, opening his jacket wide, inviting her arms to wrap around him, pulling it tight around her and she shivered and could smell the traces of tobacco on his shirt. Walking through the city streets, his hand around her, drawing her in, her voice distant, removed. His hand moved up to her shoulder and she found his waist, meeting the worn, smooth leather of his belt where her fingers lingered as they walked; soft foot falls gaining speed, signs blazing out from every angle, leading her quickly down the street, pulling her in, tighter to his side, a siren shrieking in the distance, faces passing blankly by – half lives on the periphery of a private world.

Flirting had become foreplay and she recalled each whispered word with a secret smile. The weight of his leg resting against her own, the smell of sweet whiskey and the peaty taste of it on her tongue as they kissed; the press of his hand on her thigh in the half-dark; tracing ink lines on the inside of his arm, feeling his pulse, tracking the fretwork of flowers on his skin with her fingertip; caressing vodka-filled crystal in her palm. The drinks and joint they shared hit her hard in the city streets, and she longed for the warmth of a bed and for him.

Hailing a cab he pulled her inside and slid her skirt higher, silk stockings keeping flesh from flesh, leaning across her body to pull the door tight-shut, her hand joining his. Enclosed, the radiators pumped out thick musty air tainted with engine fumes and the driver's stale cigars. She watched him again, a face half-lit by shop fronts, half-shadowed in darkness, her pulse quickening as the night raced. A shared look, fragments of light refracting red from the windscreen, lights change, and she glances at the shape of his lips defiantly waiting for hers to graze against them, laughing at her hesitation, now that they are finally away from the clamour and noise. He called out an address she didn't hear, pulling him towards her by an upturned shirt collar, he grabbed handfuls of her hair and kissed her body breathless on the vinyl seat, the cab speeding through the neon glow of taillights and streetlamps.

*

She hears the door slam and his footsteps clicking along the corridor; he is checking his collar in the hallway mirror, deleting messages from his phone. She knows it all. Each deception and every trick. The sideways glance when he speaks about his day in hurried tones, the apologies for long hours, paperwork piling up and bosses being demanding. She's made the after-hours calls to work to hear his voicemail pick up, caught late-night tubes and followed him to bars in bleak parts of town. That is was his secretary neither surprised nor shocked her. She almost pitied his lack of imagination. Objectively, yes she was pretty in the way that other women are. In a way she is not.

She selects spices and throws them in, the comforting warmth of a familiar smell enveloping her. He will swiftly head for the shower, remove his shirt and bury it deep in the laundry basket amongst his socks, t-shirts and jeans. She will find it later, press it against her face and find perfume in all the usual places, and the ache will almost certainly return. You can smell the day on someone's clothes – the office, the lunch in a busy bar, each cigarette smoked, each perfumed kiss in a quiet corridor - bodies up close, slamming against the wall.

But the smell will disappear and the ache will dissipate after subjecting the shirt to a ninety-degree wash. She will stare at the creased and misshapen collar as she shakes it from the machine, the manufactured scent of summer covering the truth. She really shouldn't iron those wrinkles in, it will spoil the shirt.

'Hello darling,' she hears herself say as she tears the skin from the onion and chops the top and bottom off in swift, sharp swipes.

'Sorry I'm late,' she hears him reply as his lips brush her cheek he reeks of stale peppermint mingled with booze and she half-turns to smile, tears springing up in her eyes, wincing at the sting.

'No problem,' the words slip from her lips easily, like the onion from her palm into the sizzling oil.

'Smells good,' he says as he always does, and she nods and throws in crushed garlic watching it turn brown. She shouldn't let it burn it will spoil the dish. It begins to shrivel and wither in the heat.

'Getting changed,' he calls on his way up the stairs.

'Yes,' she replies.

Thuds on the ceiling above; the sound of a shower. She imagines the water running down his body, every contour and line of his form as familiar as her own, the tang of citrus filling the room and clearing his head. She should turn off the heat and expire the flame. She should join him, stepping naked into the steamy warmth. She thinks of clothes being tugged off, tripping up the stairs, hands on her, hands on him; desperate. She thinks of the child beginning to grow like a secret within her. She longs for the smell of a newborn baby's hair and skin. And she imagines breathing it in, giving her life. She pours in the coconut milk, bitter spices blending with the sweetness of the liquid, and it begins to curdle and turn in the oil. She stirs it slowly, watching colours and consistencies combine and blend together again, hoping she has saved it, concentrating on the ways it looks and smells, lifting the spoon to her lips for a hesitant taste and she already knows it is spoiled.

'Almost finished,' he calls.

'Yes,' she says.

The Factory of Forgetting
By Phillip Lawrence

The Smell of Wet Concrete

She started walking after it all went wrong. She didn't see why she should sit in her flat and wait. Wait for what?

So she came to know the streets around her south London home in detail. Under low clouds and on black, damp, pavements she walked, the heath flat around her, the crows hopping on the grass oblivious to her presence. She walked towards Greenwich and caught a smell of yeast, a deep pungent rolling trail of it sweeping across the heath.

Raising her head, she took a deep draught of it in and smiled to herself: it came from the sugar refinery factory just upriver. The Thames path ran alongside it, in fact it almost went right through it. She had walked there once with Oliver, they had looked up at the sugar-filled towers and the Bladerunner spires of the refinery, belching gouts of blue flame and flickering in the night sky. And that smell: not the sweetness of sugar but the dank stench of rotten fruit.

They had gone to a restaurant and stared into each others eyes. That old, old story.

A crow jumped out of her way with a squawk as she turned to walk back to Blackheath village. The smell of the refinery made her think of her father and

Of Turpentine

She was back in her father's studio watching him paint. He stepped towards the easel very slowly and very carefully, and as he did so he selected the right colours from the palette in his left arm. With the brush now loaded (aqua marine, yellow ochre, and her favourite, burnt sienna), he applied the paint to the canvas with a small, graceful movement. Then he would step back, look hard, and repeat the whole sequence.

When he had had enough her father would dip the paintbrushes in an old jar filled with turpentine and then swirl them around, digging the colour out of the bristles until the turps was a dirty grey colour. That smell was her father, spirituous and acrid, the turps in her memory equaling his love for her. If ever, in her adult travels, she smelt the other studio smells, the varnishes he used and the oil paint itself, she was instantly a little girl again: looking up as he stepped back and stepped forwards again and again. He'd given her a random selection of his art books and she was happy to sit there for hours, flipping the pages and staring at the pictures, occasionally looking up at her father before looking back down at the book again. She said nothing. He said nothing.

She remembered being happy then.

Stray Perfume

She remembered suburban dinner parties, with her mother holding court and the smell of Beef Wellington and candles. The couples would drink wine and talk loudly and there was the occasional screech of female laughter. And their perfumes: each woman wore a powerful concoction, bought dearly at the Army and Navy store or Allders. Their perfumes met and coagulated, congealed; they filled the house until she and her sister shook their heads with wonder at the splendour of it all. How sweet it must be to be an adult.

Two things told her that Oliver was cheating on her. One was the look she saw pass between Oliver and her sister. A look filled with longing and lust.

The second came a few weeks later when she was filling the washing machine and caught a scent, a few stray molecules of perfume on the collar of one of his shirts. She checked further and it was on his cuff as well. She knew the perfume.

Mitsuko by Guerlain. Her sister wore it. It was weeks since they had seen her.

It took two hours to get the truth out of him later that evening. He left the next day.

She started pounding out his memory from the soles of her feet, leaving his poisonous residue on damp pavements, under low clouds.

The Smell of Old Dreams
By Patrick Browning

A black shadow falls across the frosted glass door of the Black Swan and the pub's dull interior takes a turn for the funereal. The pall falls across the stale interior generating a perceptible rustle, like crispy leather skin, as its patrons burrow back into the safety of their crevices.

The clock on the wall emits a dusty bong...

Gwynne Lowe's podgy mitt pushes aside the saloon door, producing a dull squeak. His pockmarked snout enters in the vanguard, twitching left and right like a St. Vitus' rabbit in the musty air, sniffing the vague scents of stagnant liqueur, fag smoke ... and dreams. His grubby forehead and jowls, clearly wanting in on the action, seep slowly in behind, sickeningly red as though embarrassed at the attention their pustulous landscape is attracting. Jostling for position in the rear comes a pair of prize cauliflower ears, keen to discern any sign of musical talent in the vicinity.

Satisfied that there isn't, the rest of Gwynne's unremarkable body pops through the doorway all at once, like the tail of a gargantuan blackhead. Resplendently dishevelled, he is clad, between highlighted mullet and croc skin boots, in a too-tight black drainpipe suit, tarnished wing-tips and a massive brass belt-buckle so tight that it seems to be staunching the flow of flab between his puffy torso and impossibly spindly legs. Not quite impossible though, for said pins manage to carry him forward to the bar, for what must be the...He gives up the calculation, the walk to the bar isn't far enough.

He props a guitar case against the oak. Behind the pumps a bored barmaid tears her attention away from a lurking paramour, who lurks so successfully that he is not mentioned for the rest of the story. Clearly piqued at this willful disrespect toward her bit-on-the-side, she sidles over toward the front of the bar, only pausing to gouge out an errant gusset with chipped pink talons.

'Can I 'elp?' She hisses, eyeing Gwynne's guitar case with suspicion.

'Get me,' he addresses her bosoms, 'the governor.' 'Get me Pete and tell him it's Gwynne.'

The barmaid remains unperturbed; her nightly battles with the Swan's slurring patrons renders her completely immune too Gwynne's surly request. She bats her thick eyelashes. 'PEEEEEETE!' Her voice peaks with a glass-rattling screech, 'There's some old bloke 'ere wants you. He's got an instrument.'

Out of thin air, a neat man of indeterminate age appears at her side. He is dressed in a white roll neck and beige slacks. The silence of his entrance is ensured by a pair of velvet slippers He seems almost aglow amidst the drab surroundings.

'Ahh. Gwynne,' he purrs, 'so nice to see you. It's been such a while.'

'Pete.' Gwynne acknowledges. 'Music on tonight? Brought my guitar.'

The landlord peers glassily at said instrument, a slight nervous tick wrinkling his otherwise smooth cheek. He refocuses on the imputed troubadour with a benign smile.

'Ah. Of course, Gwynne. We can fit you in right before The Burning Sensations. A robust rock combo - I think you'll compliment each other nicely.' He flickered not a bit as this mighty untruth was uttered. 'Mmmm. Really.'

'They 'eadlining are they?'

'No Gwynne, they're on first, er, well second now of course.' No stranger to the immutable laws that govern even the lowliest gig, the landlord tried to paper over this grave insult; 'be nice to have someone of your, erm, experience warming up the show.' He attempts to make his facial expression agree with the sounds coming out of his mouth, only failing slightly.

'I'm still up for that residency we talked about last time Pete,' Gwynne cajoles, blind optimism driving him on. 'I could do Wednesday thru Saturday nights. On a fixed contract, like. Forever.'

Forever. Gwynne uses this final word as proof of his personal commitment, which is just what the landlord fears. Visibly blanching, he recalls Gwynne Lowe's previous stints on the Swan's miniscule stage. Perennially untuned guitar, an irritating nasal whine, and worst of all his obscenely padded leather trousers, bulging and twisting horribly as Gwynne strutted his stuff. He'd had to get the smelling salts out last time, when Mrs. Pugh the cleaner accidentally caught Gwynne padding his cods in the dressing room. Poor love had a nasty turn.

Come to think of it, the worst thing about Gwynne Lowe was his appalling attitude. He had such a chip on his shoulder. Always getting drunk after his set, and heckling the other performers. It was meant to be a bit of fun for the punters, not a forum for ageing rockers to bleat about 'lack of recognition'. He cringes at his own stupidity for mentioning the residency gig the last time Gwynne had been in town. He'd only said it to get rid of the man. Forever? No chance, he would have to be firm.

'Let's see how you get on tonight eh Gwynne? There's lot's of new talent around these days...' Sensing this might be going too far, he tries another tack: 'And the brewery's strapped these days, we'd not be able to pay you.'

Sensing defeat, and another interminable season of pointless gigs in empty pubs and clubs, hauling his puckered arse and equipment around behind him, Gwynne grunts and stomps away from the bar.

'Tom'll be round to make sure you're plugged in and sound-checked in about half an hour.' the landlord says from somewhere beneath the bar as he fumbles for his earplugs.

'Yeah. Whatever.'

The trouble with Gwynne Lowe was that he was completely devoid of musical talent, and in that peculiar way common to those of his ilk, had a deep conviction of the exact opposite. As a gangly teen he'd taken time out from his own woefully inadequate fretboard masturbation to occasionally roadie for a bunch of beer-headed blues bands. Canvey, Wycombe, the Frome folk-jazz jamboree, you name it. He'd seen some action. Then one night he got his first taste of the big time. A band called The Orange and Green Psychedelic Dream Team had been booked at the Frindsbury Extra Blues Jam. They were a new group and rapidly attracting a big following of heads. On their opening night however, their lead guitarist had taken a strange concoction of LSD and Benylin, and decided to quit music and live up a tree near Ely Cathedral. In the right place at the right time, Gwynne got himself a gig. Faced with bankruptcy, the Dream Team's manager took one look at the spotty gimp in front of him and thought what the hell.

Not even the Seventies' prevailing trend for widdly, interminable guitar frottage in could mask Gwynne's basic lack of talent. As soon as the Dream Team's tour finished, Gwynne was told, in no uncertain terms, to fuck off. Undaunted by this setback, and fuelled by a drug swollen self-obsession, he took matters into his own precious hands. Got himself a manager - later to become his wife - a solo album, a curly mullet; he was set.

Then came the problems. Divorce proceedings cleared him out of money; a hastily recorded solo project designed to bridge the financial gap foundered; cocaine and alcohol did the rest. Gwynne ended up doing covers in pubs and clubs within a radius from his knackered caravan dictated solely by his spluttering Vauxhall Princess. After a bit of a bender following a particularly disastrous show in a trucker bar near Romford, he'd found himself in need of a quick escape. Well over the limit, he'd nodded out whilst driving up his own driveway, totalling car and caravan in true rock and roll style. That gave him a turn. He quit the hard stuff after that.

But still his ego kept him at it. Traipsing between each boozer with a music licence, he gradually worked up a circuit that kept body and soul together. Impervious to the boldest of criticism, but strangely susceptible to the most insincere praise, he'd grasped the landlord of the Black Swan's misguided suggestion about a residency with both metaphorical hands, which like his physical ones, were heavily callused. Picking up his battered guitar he felt a surge of the old Gwynne axe-magic. He'd show 'em. He'd do his extended version of 'Freebird,' with extra hip-wiggling. He'd do 'Touch Me', that always got them going. And he'd do Purple Haze, with full floor-thrashing and dribbling as an encore. They'd give him the residency. They'd give it him and apologise for not having done so before. That fucking barmaid. She'd ditch that spotty poof and come begging when she saw some good ol' Gwynne Lowe mojo…

*

Gwynne Lowe comes to a supine rest after his last ecstatic convulsion. The last fractured wails of the overloaded P.A slowly ebb, and he opens his eyes to survey his adoring audience. As this now only consists of the landlord - blissfully unaware of the preceding cacophony due to heavy aural muffling - and a terrified dachshund, he gets up and dusts himself off. Wiping the sweat from his brow and adjusting the padding round his nadgers Gwynne slowly gets to his feet. Collecting some of the larger fragments of guitar and chucking them into his case, he prepares to leave the stage. Looking up, he meets the landlord's eye. It's not encouraging.
'How about just Mondays?' Gwynne pleads?
'Sorry Gwynne. No residency.'

Thrusting on his tattered jacket, Gwynne Lowe makes for the door, his guitar case now rattling in a sinister fashion, a few strings hanging out of its hinges. Without looking back, he shoulders his way through the pub door, aiming to slam it smartly behind him, but only succeeding in catching his foot.
'This place fucking stinks!'
And he's gone.
Following his pathetic exit with interest, the landlord's benign smile lights once again across his sharp, handsome features. The dachshund looks at him, then the door, then makes a run for it. A thick stillness slowly descends and it is evident that there will be no more music this evening. The clock has wound on mysteriously to Time. The sterling barkeep takes his large key over to the door and locks it, shooting the bolts home with a quiet trepidation. He walks back to the bar and dims the lights. It's very quiet. The lingering smell of failure has departed.